to Morgan

THE SECRET
OF THE
CROCODILES

# KAREN WALLACE

*Karen Wallace*

**SIMON AND SCHUSTER**

First published in Great Britain by Simon & Schuster UK Ltd, 2005
A Viacom company

1 3 5 7 9 10 8 6 4 2

Simon & Schuster UK Ltd
Africa House
64-78 Kingsway
London WC2B 6AH

A CIP catalogue record for this book is available from the British Library

ISBN 0 689 87483 9

Typeset by SX Composing DTP, Rayleigh, Essex
Printed by Cox & Wyman, Reading, Berkshire

LADY VIOLET WINTERS

CAIRO
1902

Also by
# KAREN WALLACE

Raspberries on the Yangtze
Climbing a Monkey Puzzle Tree
Wendy
The Unrivalled Spangles

Look out for Lady Violet's next adventure.
The Man with Tiger Eyes.
coming soon.

Margaret. with love – and thanks

# ONE

Lady Violet Winters leaned over the rails of the steamship *Lara* and stared down at the bright turquoise waters of the Mediterranean Sea. A hot gusty breeze blew up the fine lawn skirt of her green-and-yellow striped dress. Violet looked behind her. The deck was empty except for her governess, Madame Amelie Poisson, who was asleep in a bathchair on the deck behind her. The book of Latin odes she had been reading lay open in her hand, its pages flapping like so many fish. Violet smiled to herself. Madame Poisson was the perfect governess. She was always either indisposed or asleep. Violet called her her 'dear codfish' because she looked just like one. Amelie Poisson had silver-grey skin, a full lower lip and the popping-out eyes of a codfish. They even had whiskers in common!

Violet checked once more to be sure she was alone, then she closed her eyes and let the warm breeze fill her skirts so they billowed out around her ankles.

It was blissful, and impossible to imagine that barely two weeks ago, she had been sitting at her desk in the schoolroom on the top floor of her home at Number 2, Portman Square.

Violet remembered that grey, wet afternoon exactly. It had been three weeks before Christmas and she had been feeling dull and out of sorts. Usually Violet looked forward to this time of year. Her mother, Lady Eleanor, always took her out shopping for presents along the brightly lit streets around Piccadilly and Oxford Circus; it was their custom to look at all the gorgeous window displays. Then her mother took her to an exquisite teashop in St James' Street and, over a cup of Earl Grey tea and a slice of Battenburg cake, they discussed the merits of each window display and finally agreed on an overall winner. It was one of the few things Violet and her mother enjoyed doing together because, on the whole, they were interested in completely different things. Lady Eleanor loved dressing in beautiful clothes and entertaining important people at dinner parties and receptions. Violet didn't really mind *what* she wore, as long as it wasn't too frilly or too tight. But most of all she wanted to go to university to study. Her father had gone to Cambridge and was recognised as having one of the finest minds of his generation. It was Violet's ambition to follow in his footsteps. Furthermore, while Lady Eleanor was beautiful and slender with fine blonde hair and pale-green eyes, Violet could not be considered pretty. She was tall for her age and her hair was dark and curly. She had a strong, square face with a large, wide mouth. But her eyes were the colour of lapis lazuli. 'Quite the most extraordinary blue, darling,' her mother would murmur. 'From my Irish side, of course.' Sometimes her father would catch her eye and wink. They both knew that her colouring came irrefutably from his family.

\*

That afternoon in the schoolroom, Violet had stabbed her pen on her blotter so hard that she broke the nib. It was no wonder she was dreading Christmas. At the last moment, her mother had insisted that her father's aunt, Great-aunt Millicent, spend Christmas with them in London. Much as she tried not to, Violet heartily detested her great-aunt. She was overbearing, snobbish and nosey. Worst of all, since Violet was an only-child and Great-aunt Millicent had no children of her own, it was impossible to avoid her attention. And Great-aunt Millicent seemed to believe she had a right to interfere in every aspect of Violet's life.

Violet stared out at the pouring rain and sighed. It would be far better to be imprisoned in a crumbling castle like the heroines in the gothic novels she loved reading than to face Great-aunt Millicent's incessant questioning over the tea-table.

At that moment, Madame Poisson pulled open the schoolroom door. '*Violette, ma chère*, quickly, change your dress! Your father and mother want to see you immediately!'

Five minutes later, Violet wore her favourite blue

velvet dress and knocked on the heavy oak door of her father's study.

Her father's voice was unusually deep. 'Come in.'

As soon as she stepped into the room, Violet knew that something serious had happened. Her mother was sitting on the sofa, turning her rings round and round on her fingers. Her father was standing behind his desk, looking distractedly out of the window. He turned as she entered.

'Violet, my dear,' said Lord Percy. 'Sad news, I'm afraid.' His lined, handsome face was drawn. 'News has just reached us that Great-aunt Millicent has died.'

Violet immediately felt a great feeling of guilt wash over her. Only ten minutes ago she had been wishing herself in a dungeon rather than face her great-aunt over tea. She blushed and tried to say something, but nothing came out of her mouth.

Lord Percy smiled kindly at his daughter as if he understood what she was thinking. It had always been his opinion that his aunt had been born at her own insistence and had started handing out orders to the midwife the moment she drew breath.

Nevertheless, Great-aunt Millicent – dragon that she was – had also meant well, and he was sad that she had died.

He picked up the letter and walked over to where Violet was standing. Violet's eyes fell on the paper. She recognised her great-aunt's slanted, copperplate writing. Her father put his hand on her shoulder. 'She made a request particularly for you.'

Despite herself, Violet's heart sank. Whatever the request was, she knew she would have to agree to her great-aunt's wishes. 'What is it, Father?'

Lord Percy shook his head as if slightly perplexed. 'She asks that we spend Christmas travelling in Egypt.'

The room was silent except for the ticking of the carriage clock on her father's desk and the endless trickle of rain against the windowpane. Violet was so stunned all she could do was stare at her black patent shoes. It was so much the opposite of what she had been expecting to hear. 'I don't understand,' she said finally.

Lord Percy smiled at his thirteen-year-old daughter. 'Nor do I, but your mother is keen and frankly –' he looked out at the pouring rain '– I would be happy to get away from this infernal weather.'

'Sit beside me, darling,' said Lady Eleanor in her rich, smooth voice. She patted the seat beside her. Violet sat down. She was expecting her mother to discuss the etiquette of mourning clothes. Again she was wrong. Her mother cleared her throat. 'You see something *else* has happened that is going to affect us all.'

Her father sat down on the arm of the sofa and began to speak.

And that was the first time that Violet heard about a young American called Garth Hudson.

'A dime for your thoughts, LV,' said a voice, in a teasing, twangy accent. 'Or maybe they're worth a dollar.'

Violet turned to the auburn-haired boy standing beside her. She had known him less than a month and yet now it was impossible to imagine life without him. Part of Garth was the brother she had always wanted and part of him was the companion that made her life in the schoolroom bearable. But the best thing of all was that he was so *un-English*. So many of the conventions she took for granted, he questioned. Not in a rude way, of course. He just shrugged his shoulders and rolled his eyes. Then he told her another story of hunting deer in the woods or cutting holes in frozen lakes and fishing for trout. Violet was thrilled at the hugeness and wildness of the land on his side of the ocean, and in return she tried to explain the bizarre intricacies of her own world. It was like comparing an exquisitely-made dolls' house to a sturdy log cabin.

'Thoughts are always sixpence, Garth,' said Violet grinning. 'No matter how important they are.'

Garth grinned back. 'Don't sell yourself short, LV. For all *you* know they might be worth a sovereign – and that's a lot of cash, no matter *who's* counting.'

Violet laughed. She couldn't believe that her parents had been worried that she would be jealous of him. She thought again about that rainy afternoon and her father's voice as he tried to find the right words to explain what had happened . . .

*

'You see, Violet, Garth's father, Conrad, was an old friend from Cambridge. After we left university, he went to New York to set up his business.' Lord Percy had cleared his throat and smoothed an invisible crease in his impeccably-tailored pinstripe suit. 'We kept in close contact, of course, and worked together occasionally. When I agreed to be Garth's guardian, well, I never thought—'

'He is, by all accounts, quite sophisticated for an American,' said Lady Eleanor quickly. 'He has attended the best schools and will continue his education at your father's old college.'

'What happened to his mother?' asked Violet. 'Has he no relatives in America?'

'Garth's mother died in childbirth,' said Lord Percy. 'He has been brought up for the past fourteen years by Conrad's unmarried sister.' He paused, and Violet could sense that her father was remembering something particular. 'Conrad was most insistent that if anything should happen to him, Garth should come immediately to England and begin a new life with us.'

For the third time that afternoon, Violet was lost for words.

'You won't mind, darling, will you?' asked Lady Eleanor anxiously.

'No. No,' replied Violet quickly. 'I'd be delighted to have some company.' She paused. 'Will he come to Egypt with us?'

'Of course,' said Lord Percy. 'His ship arrives in Liverpool in two days' time. We'll leave for Egypt as soon as arrangements can be made.'

'Look!' cried Garth suddenly. Violet was jerked out of her reverie. She followed his finger pointing into the water. 'Dolphins! Do you see them?'

A few yards away from the side of the ship, five dolphins soared out of the water. Violet stared at their sleek, silver bodies and the bright, beady eyes above the smiling line of their mouths. They leapt in and out of the bow wave of the steamer as if it was a ride at the fairground.

Violet shrieked with delight. It was the most thrilling thing she had ever seen in her life.

'It's like they're trying to tell us something,' she

shouted, above the rumble of the ship's engines.

Garth nodded excitedly. He was just as thrilled as she was. 'But what?'

'That we're going to have the best adventure *ever* in Egypt!' cried Violet. She spun around until her skirts blew up around her knees. Then, out of the corner of her eye, she saw Madame Poisson moving towards them with a stern expression in her watery eyes. Violet knew she was going to get scolded for showing her ankles. 'Codfish alert,' she cried, as she bunched up the billowing cloth and held it down against her legs.

Garth saw the look on the governess's face. Girls' clothes were a mystery to him but he knew there were layers and layers of them and that compared to what Violet had to wear, his short cotton jacket and baggy trousers were ten times cooler. 'Leave her to me,' he said quickly. 'I'll dazzle her with my newly-acquired French.'

He quickly crossed the deck and stopped Madame Poisson in her tracks. A moment later, Violet heard her governess's squawking laughter and watched as Garth made soaring and diving movements with his hands. The word *dauphin* floated towards her and Madame Poisson's face lit up with delight.

Violet smiled to herself. That was one of the things she loved about her dear codfish. Amelie Poisson was passionate about learning, and she was a brilliant teacher. The fact that she was a bad traveller suited Violet perfectly. While the codfish had spent most of the trip lying down in her cabin with the curtains drawn over the porthole, she and Garth had set up a contest to see who could make up the best stories about all the people in the first-class saloon. So far both of them had agreed on a tie.

Violet looked quickly at the little gold watch she wore on a chain around her neck. It was almost half past four. Every day it was agreed that she would meet her parents for tea. She walked across the shiny teak deck and opened the door to the inside of the ship. She turned to see if Madame had noticed. But she hadn't. In fact, her codfish was obviously so enthralled with Garth's description of the dolphins, she had forgotten all about scolding Violet.

*

Violet stood in the first-class cabin she shared with Madame Poisson and stared at herself in the long wall-mirror. She had chosen her clothes carefully for her tea-time meeting. Not so much with her father in mind – Lord Percy Winters was usually keen to discuss books, and more recently Egyptian history, with his daughter. It was Lady Eleanor whom Violet intended to impress. She had noticed that her mother was beginning to blame Madame Poisson for her apparent lack of interest in helping her charge acquire the sophisticated polish that Lady Eleanor believed was required in society. Once, she had even accused Madame Poisson of turning her daughter into a 'fuddy-duddy blue-stocking'. The idea of going to university was perfectly appalling to Lady Eleanor, and Violet knew her mother had been looking for an excuse to relieve Madame Poisson of her duties: 'Violet, if you do not make more of an effort with your appearance, I shall throw that useless French fish into the Channel and let her *swim* back to Cherbourg.' A dramatic flourish of her mother's long, white, elegant arm and a jangling of bracelets always accompanied the last part of the sentence.

Luckily for Violet, however, her father took a different view. He supported her ambition to go to university.

Violet knew the solution lay with her. All she had to do was to take a more careful interest in her clothes. Appearances were everything to Lady Eleanor.

Now Violet turned slowly in front of the mirror. Surely her mother would approve this time! Violet had tied back her hair and fixed it with combs and a bright-blue ribbon. She wore a plain white, pin-tucked blouse and an embroidered blue waistcoat over a dark-red, panelled skirt. As a final touch, she pinned a lapis lazuli brooch at her neck. She knew it would complement the colour of her eyes.

It was almost five o'clock. Violet closed the door carefully behind her. As she ran along the corridor, she caught sight of Garth and Madame Poisson in deep conversation. Violet tried not to feel jealous. She was sure that they would be talking about something much more interesting than the latest London gossip or big-game hunting on the Nile, which were the main topics of conversation in the first-class tea lounge.

It wasn't fair. Her parents didn't insist that Garth join them every day and they allowed him more freedom than she had. He could go anywhere on the boat. She had to stay in the first-class section.

Violet kicked open a door to make herself feel better. Then she took a deep breath and walked demurely into the palm-fringed white-and-gold saloon, where her parents were sitting in a circle of other guests.

'Violet, darling! How lovely you look!' Lady Eleanor smiled up from her chair at the centre of the circle. She lifted her face, and Violet dutifully kissed her mother's smooth, white cheek. Lady Eleanor's complexion was considered by many to be one of the Seven Wonders of the World. She never went out in the sun without a veil and a broad-brimmed hat, and covered her face in strange creams at night. 'You remember Count Kapolski, of course.'

Violet stared into the almost colourless eyes of a blond-haired man. She had taken an instant dislike to him at the beginning of the voyage, though she couldn't explain why. It was more of an instinctive reaction. His manners were impeccable, but there was a coldness about him that made it seem as if he was only playing a part. Apparently he was some minor Russian aristocrat and something of an art collector, so her mother had placed her next to him at dinner on the first night.

Not only did Count Kapolski make Violet's skin crawl, but the geranium-scented hair oil he used had a particularly pungent smell that made her gag. He had told her he was a big-game hunter and travelled the world to find and kill as many exotic animals as he could find. It was the thrill of the chase, he'd explained, with a patronising smile. It was unlike anything else. Then he had informed her that he had shot more tigers last year in India than anyone else, and now that he was in Egypt he intended to repeat the achievement. This time he was after the Nile crocodile.

Count Kapolski's voice had been high and boasting, and when he spoke his delicate, almost womanish, hands moved constantly. As he had listed his successes, his mouth had spread into a thin-lipped, self-satisfied smile.

16

He was the most repulsive man Violet had ever met.

All the time she had been seated next to him, Violet could only think of the moment when she could politely turn to the person on her other side. When at last she was able to break away, she found herself listening to the family history of a deaf Irish peer who spat out his food as he spoke. Apparently his family had a third cousin once removed who was related to the present King Edward VII.

At the other end of the table, she had watched Garth – who could usually talk the hind legs off a donkey – try again and again to draw the Countess Maria Kapolski into any kind of conversation. But despite his efforts, the woman's heavy face remained expressionless.

Towards the end of that first dinner, Violet and Garth had exchanged glances. It was time for some amateur dramatics. Anything to get them out of the room. A few minutes later, they both feigned sunstroke.

It was a creditable piece of acting and Lord

Percy had agreed, with a knowing gleam in his eye, that they be allowed to leave the table. Violet wasn't surprised he had agreed so readily. On one side, he had a dowager duchess with pronounced views on hunting with dogs and, on the other, a carpet magnate's wife who had endless trouble with her servants. Violet could tell from her father's face that the evening had become rather tiresome for him.

Now, as the last day of their sea journey approached, Violet sat down at the edge of the circle around the tea-table and hoped Garth would appear. She wrinkled her nose as the smell of geranium oil wafted past her. To her disgust, Count Kapolski laid his cool, slimy fingers on her wrist.

'Lady Violet,' he murmured. 'What a pleasant surprise.' He fixed her with his colourless eyes. 'I trust you have recovered from the sun's excesses?'

Violet forced herself to laugh. 'Oh, completely, Count Kapolski!' She stared at her hands to avoid looking at him. 'Indeed, I have made good use of my time at sea.'

'Reading poetry, no doubt.'

'In fact, I have become something of an expert in anthropology.'

Even as she spoke, Violet regretted her response. It was silly and arrogant, and that was a mistake.

'She means we've been making up stories about everyone in first class,' said Garth in his easy drawl, behind her.

Violet turned around and glared at Garth. She knew her face had gone bright red. How could he be so stupid?

'How very *American* of you both,' said the Count, in an unpleasant voice. He turned away as he spoke, so Garth didn't have a chance to reply.

Now it was Garth's turn to blush angrily. 'How dare he sneer like that?'

'When are you going to learn?' hissed Violet. She glared at him. 'You can't be cocky with people like that. They always make it sound as if you're being rude.'

'He's a pig,' said Garth, under his breath.

Violet rolled her eyes. She was determined not to let the Count spoil their last evening on board.

'Come on,' she said, in a bad New York accent. 'Forget it. Tell me something new.'

Garth forced himself to overcome his irritation. Violet was right. It was his own fault. He had to learn to keep his mouth shut. A smile flickered across his face. 'Something new *has* happened,' he said quickly. 'I was going to tell you earlier, then fish-face—'

'Codfish.'

'Haddock-head – who cares?' Garth walked towards a spray of palm leaves between two bamboo chairs. Violet stood up and followed him. She turned once to glance across at her mother. Lady Eleanor smiled and Violet knew that the trouble she had taken over her clothes had been worthwhile. Her mother was pleased with her. Now her time was her own. She turned back and sat down beside Garth.

'So, what's happened?' she asked.

Garth motioned her nearer, and Violet listened as he told her how he had been prowling around the deck at midnight with a young man he'd met in second class called Nicholas Etherington, and how they had seen a mysterious woman appear by the rails.

Violet had already heard about Nicholas Etherington from Garth. He seemed to be a young man from a good family, which made it odd that he was travelling second class. But at least he had a cabin to himself, so while Violet had been shut up with Madame Poisson, memorising Latin odes, Nicholas had been teaching Garth Arabic. When Violet asked Garth what his new friend was doing in Cairo, Garth didn't know. He had asked in a roundabout way, but Nicholas was unwilling to say more than that his business was something to do with importing and exporting.

'This woman was wearing a veil,' said Garth, his voice rising. As he spoke his hands outlined the shape of a veil hanging over his face. '*At night!*'

For some reason, at that moment Violet looked up and saw the Count staring at them.

Garth didn't notice and went on talking quickly. 'Then a gust of wind blew up and I saw her face.'

'Garth!' whispered Violet, to silence him.

'It was really peculiar,' said Garth, not hearing

the warning in her voice. 'The woman looked as if she had been chiselled out of marble. But you know what was strangest of all?' Despite himself, his eyes strayed across the room towards Count Kapolski.

'Don't look at him,' said Violet, urgently. 'He's watching you.'

'So what?' replied Garth, remembering the earlier insult. 'It was him I saw last night. He appeared out of nowhere and the woman passed him a note.'

'Tea, milady?' A white-gloved steward bowed in front of them.

'Yes, please,' said Violet quickly. 'Two.'

'Milk and sugar?'

'Lots,' said Garth. 'And some chocolate cake, please.'

Garth sank his teeth into a huge piece of dark, rich chocolate cake. 'So, what do you want to do?' he asked, his mouth full. 'We could follow them when we get to Cairo.'

'Maybe.' Violet bit into her own piece of cake. 'The thing is, I heard the Count tell Father that he and the Countess were leaving immediately for

Luxor.' She pulled a face. 'Apparently there are more crocodiles further up the Nile.'

The truth was, she didn't care much whether she ever saw Count Kapolski again.

Garth read her mind from the look on her face. 'Yeah, he is a nasty piece of work – that's for sure.' He reached out for a second piece of cake. 'Tell you what: Nicholas Etherington says he'll take us around the bazaar in Cairo. We're bound to have some sort of adventure there.'

Violet sighed. 'Father would never allow it. Nicholas Etherington is a stranger.'

Garth looked up. 'No, he's not. He told me this morning that his father knows your father.'

'What? Then why didn't he introduce himself? Why didn't he travel first class?'

'How should I know?' replied Garth. 'Maybe the company was better.'

Violet looked across the room. 'The Count's still staring at us,' she said, in a low voice.

Garth grinned. 'These foreigners have no manners,' he said, in a loud, English accent.

'It's not funny.' Violet shivered for the first time

in almost two weeks. 'I'm sure he saw you telling me about the veiled lady.'

Garth shrugged. 'If he's going on to Luxor, he can't do anything about it.'

Violet shivered again. She couldn't explain why. She changed the subject. 'Tell me more about Nicholas Etherington.'

# TWO

'Papa,' said Violet, as they stood in the shade of the white stone portico at Cairo station. 'I'd like you to meet Nicholas Etherington. He was, uh, travelling with Garth.' She swallowed nervously. 'You know his father, Sir Edward.'

On the train up from Alexandria, while her parents were dining in the restaurant car and Madame was nursing a headache in a darkened sleeping cabin, Nicholas Etherington had joined them in their private compartment and confirmed his offer to take Violet and Garth – and Madame, of course – to the covered bazaar in Cairo. 'It's an extraordinary place,' he'd told them. 'Like another world.'

25

From what Garth had told her the day before, Violet knew that Nicholas's parents had lived in Cairo when he was a child. His father had been something to do with the Embassy but had now gone into business in London.

Lord Percy Winters smiled down at his daughter. 'Of course I know Sir Edward!' he cried. He shook Nicholas firmly by the hand. 'Dear boy! Why on earth didn't you join us on the steamer?' Then, not waiting for an answer, he said, 'Garth tells me that you have been teaching him some Arabic.'

Nicholas nodded. 'He's a gifted linguist, sir.'

Garth grinned. 'Not as good as you.'

Nicholas smiled shyly.

He didn't *look* like a businessman, thought Violet. There was something bumbling and uncertain about his movements. Yet the expression in his brown eyes was quick and alert.

'I would be happy to teach Violet some words too, if she would like to learn.'

'Oh, yes please!' replied Violet. She was furious that Garth could already make himself understood in the language, while she couldn't speak a word.

'Sadly, we will not have the pleasure of your company for long,' replied Sir Percy, smiling at Nicholas. 'We are only staying in Cairo for a few days over Christmas.'

'Then allow me to make the best of the time you have.' Nicholas bowed. 'With your permission I will take Violet and Garth to the covered bazaar. It is an extraordinary place and I know it well.'

Violet held her breath. Luckily her mother was still overseeing the unloading of their baggage. Lady Eleanor distrusted crowds of foreigners as a matter of principle, so it was likely she would object to the excursion.

'I would be delighted if you would accompany Violet and Garth,' replied Lord Percy. He paused. 'And Madame, of course.'

'Of course,' said Nicholas quickly. 'I shall look forward to it.' He winked at Violet. 'And we'll teach you some Arabic on the way.'

Lord Percy laughed. 'We're staying at Shepheard's. I would be honoured if you would join us for dinner.'

Nicholas's face lit up at the kindness of the offer. 'I'd be delighted, sir.'

At that moment, Lady Eleanor leaned out of a covered carriage drawn by two white donkeys. Their bridles were decorated with tassels and brass bells, which tinkled when the donkeys waggled their head to shake off the flies.

'Darling!' cried Lady Eleanor from behind the veil of a wide-brimmed hat, which was in danger of getting wedged in the window. 'Do hurry! I can't bear another moment in this heat.'

In an open cart behind her, a pale-faced Madame sat nervously, surrounded by a mountain of luggage.

'May we go with Madame?' asked Violet. She knew her mother would want to get to the hotel as quickly as possible. 'I don't mind sitting in the sun.'

'Certainly,' replied her father. He looked at the little French woman's white face. 'I suggest, Madame, that you join Her Ladyship and me.' He turned. 'Nicholas, I would be obliged if you would accompany Violet and Garth.' A glance passed between them and Violet felt her heart thump in her chest. Her father was usually very reserved – she had never known him so relaxed in the presence of a young man he barely knew.

She watched his face as Nicholas handed Madame down from the cart and helped her into the covered trap beside Lady Eleanor. Once again her father's eyes met Nicholas's in an easy acknowledgement, and suddenly Violet was sure they knew each other far better than she or Garth had been led to believe. Perhaps Lord Percy had known Nicholas was aboard the *Lara* all along. For even though Garth was given more freedom than she was, her parents would never have allowed him to visit a strange man in his cabin. Violet closed her eyes against the heat and the noise. Why on earth hadn't she realised before? Of course, it would never have occurred to Garth. Americans were more accepting of people from different backgrounds. She tried to make herself think what all this could possibly mean, but she had no idea and now they were off. The two parties pulled out into the sand-beaten street. There were people everywhere. It was like walking into an ants' nest under a bright, beating sun.

Violet recognised Shepheard's Hotel from her father's description back in London. At the time, it had sounded impossibly exotic. A five-storey building painted a pale apricot, it had a huge stone terrace dotted with palm trees which ran the length of the hotel and looked out over the busy street. In front of the terrace, all along the wide pavement, snake-charmers and conjurors performed to passers-by, while everywhere men and small boys sold trinkets piled high on trays in front of them. Egyptian women dressed in dark veils walked alongside ladies dressed in the latest French fashions. Men in striped linen suits and boater hats passed Turkish merchants wearing flowing emerald coats and yellow silk under-tunics. Violet looked at the woven rattan chairs and tables on the terrace and decided she would take tea there as often as possible.

'There are enormous stone baths underneath the hotel,' Nicholas told them as their cart stopped in front of the main doors and a footman, dressed in white with a black fez, stepped forward to help them down into the street. 'The water is quite clean and wonderfully cold.'

Garth turned to Violet. 'I do believe I'm in danger of overheating!'

'Me, too!' Violet jumped onto the street and looked up at the hotel. At the very top were half a dozen small attic windows. 'I hope our rooms are up there!'

Madame appeared beside them. '*Violette! Garth!*' she cried. 'Calm yourselves, please!'

But neither Garth nor Violet was listening.

They ran up the smooth stone steps of the hotel into the echoing entrance hall. Violet gasped. She had never seen anything like it. The room was huge and so high their voices echoed. Enormous fans hung down from the ceiling like chandeliers, their long, black blades turning slowly through the scented air. Beautifully-woven hangings covered the walls, and the floors were spread with glossy Turkish carpets. It looked like a palace out of *The Arabian Nights.*

'Your rooms are on the top floor,' said Lord Percy, joining them. 'A bit of a climb but the view is wonderful, I'm told.' He smiled at his daughter's bright, glistening face. 'I'll suggest Madame takes you both for a dip in the baths.' He turned. Madame was coming towards them. She looked hot and flustered and waved her hand like a fan in front of her face. Lord Percy winked at Violet. 'A cold splash is particularly expeditious for agitated French governesses.'

Before Violet could reply, Garth spoke. 'Lord Percy! I had never imagined such a wonderful place.'

Lord Percy laughed at his ward's obvious excitement. 'Nicholas had to leave but asked me to let you know that he will meet you on the terrace at four o'clock.' He nodded to a porter to take their luggage upstairs. 'I shall see you both at dinner.'

Ten minutes later, Violet stared out of the garret window of her bedroom at the top of the hotel. It was a view from a dream. Over the top of the huge palm trees that shaded the gardens, she saw minarets and square towers with roof terraces. In the distance, a woman dressed from head to foot in a white veil appeared on top of one of the towers.

Violet stared as the woman scattered what must have been birdseed. Seconds later, a flock of white doves flew down onto the roof terrace.

There was a childish squeak of excitement and Violet realised with a start that it had come from her own mouth. She jumped up and down and clapped her hands with delight. She watched entranced as the veiled woman bent down and picked up one of the birds in her hands.

Violet's imagination soared as she thought of stories to tell Garth. Perhaps the woman was suffering from a broken heart. Or perhaps she was married against her will and kept a prisoner in the tower. She knew from her own reading that Arab women had arranged marriages and some never left their husband's house for fear of meeting another man's eyes. Violet watched as the woman picked up a dove and cradled it. A shiver of horror crawled over her skin. It was impossible to imagine living a life like that!

She turned away from the window and stared at the woven hangings on the wall and the brass lamp swinging from the ceiling. Even her bed looked exotic, with the fine net draped over it to keep out insects. She held out her skirt and danced around the room like a princess in a fairy tale.

And to think it was only two days till Christmas! There was a knock on the door. A young Arab boy in the hotel's uniform stood in the hallway, holding an enormous white towel. 'Please you come to the water plunge, Missie. French lady and young sir wait there.'

Sir Percy was right. A dip in the icy water did Madame a world of good. When Nicholas Etherington walked across the front terrace to keep his four o'clock appointment, she practically jumped out of her chair to greet him.

Half an hour later, after a refreshing glass of mint tea, they set off down the street. Soon they were in the narrow cobbled streets of the bazaar.

Nicholas had spoken the truth. It was like a different world. Matting was slung from the tops of the houses so the light on the ground was shady and dappled. The houses themselves were narrow, and finely-carved like birdcages. In every doorway, a market seller squatted behind an open chest, selling everything from brooches to spices to rolls of shining cloth. But it was the people that amazed

Violet most. She saw servants running errands in baggy trousers and braided jackets, and thin-faced Arabs dressed in flowing brown and white robes with shawls twisted around their foreheads.

'They're from the desert,' Nicholas explained. 'All those layers of clothes actually keep them cooler in the sun.'

An enormous Turkish merchant with a hooked nose strode past them in a bright-pink tunic, with an outer coat made of black silk. He wore a dark-purple sash around his huge middle. He nodded at Nicholas and shouted out a greeting.

Violet found herself staring into the face of a wiry man with what looked like a bloated goat slung around his neck. Its front and back legs were criss-crossed on either side of his head. Where the goat's head had once been was a large, shiny brass tap.

Violet couldn't believe what she was seeing and her jaw dropped. Beside her, Garth burst out laughing. 'Glass of water, milady?'

'What?'

'He's a water-seller,' said Garth.

'How do you know?' asked Violet, suddenly cross that Garth already knew more than she did.

'I watched him sell it.'

It was a fair answer and Violet felt idiotic for being cross. 'I wonder what it tastes like.'

Garth pulled a face. 'Disgusting, probably.'

'It's not that bad, actually,' said Nicholas, who had been speaking French to Madame all the while. He turned down a narrow alley. 'This way!'

'Where are we going?' asked Violet.

'Madame Poisson tells me she has an interest in scarabs,' replied Nicholas. He bowed and Violet was pleased to see her codfish look so happy. 'I know a good dealer called Ahmed.'

'What are scarabs?' asked Violet, then frowned. It seemed all she could do was ask questions.

Nicholas smiled. 'They're Egyptian brooches shaped like scarab beetles.' He pointed to trays of jewellery on every doormat. 'These men are selling fakes.'

'They look old to me,' said Violet, staring at the tarnished-looking brooches.

'That's because they feed them to chickens and

36

turkeys first,' said Madame Poisson, proudly. 'Nicholas told me.'

Violet frowned. She didn't understand what the codfish was talking about, but she didn't want to ask another question.

'The birds' stomach acids do a better job than a forger ever could,' explained Nicholas kindly. He smiled at Violet. Immediately she felt her irritation disappear. 'Now, who would like some lemonade?'

Everyone was thirsty. Violet watched as Nicholas hailed a lemonade-seller carrying a wooden pole with a row of brass cups hanging off it. A heavy jug was propped in the crook of his elbow. Nicholas put a couple of coins in the man's hand.

Violet sipped at the lemonade. It was sweet but completely refreshing.

Madame drank her lemonade in one gulp. Violet couldn't believe her eyes. She had never seen her codfish gulp anything, ever. It seemed Egypt was working a magical spell on everyone.

A few minutes later, they stood in a small square, surrounded by jewellery-sellers. Madame shrieked with delight and immediately ran off towards a man wearing a scarlet fez, who stood lazily behind a table which glittered with shiny brooches.

'I've never seen my governess so excited,' said Violet to Nicholas. 'You should take us to the bazaar more often.'

As she spoke, she saw Garth stare across the little square with a puzzled expression. He turned to Violet. 'I thought you said that horrible Count and his wife were going straight up to Luxor?'

'They were,' said Violet. 'I saw them board the train at Cairo. Mama insisted on saying goodbye.'

'Well, he must have jumped off as soon as you left the platform.' Garth jerked his head sideways and both Violet and Nicholas followed his gaze.

A nasty, sick feeling passed through Violet. Half hidden in the shadows was the Count, talking rapidly to a man who looked liked a merchant of some sort. He had the sharp-nosed look of a rat and an unpleasant greedy shine to his face.

'Follow me,' said Nicholas in a new, grim voice. 'And whatever you do, don't turn round to look at him.'

Violet exchanged glances with Garth, but neither

of them spoke and they both did as they were told. Nevertheless, they all saw the two men turn into a doorway just off the square. Nicholas frowned.

'So, what's going on?' asked Garth, munching a sugared nut from a bag he had bought off a street pedlar.

'It's most peculiar,' muttered Nicholas. He frowned again.

'*What* is?' asked Violet.

'That merchant. He's a . . .' Nicholas paused and turned to Violet. 'I don't want to offend you.'

Violet stared at him. 'I'm only offended if you treat me like a child.' Suddenly she thought of the man's nasty-looking face and an idea straight out of an adventure story sprang into her mind. 'That fat man's a slave-trader, isn't he?'

'Yes,' blurted Nicholas, astonished by her bluntness.

Violet went white. 'He isn't really?'

'I'm afraid he is,' said Nicholas reluctantly. 'His name is Gumrhaddin and he deals in people, just like these traders deal in jewellery or –' Nicholas shrugged and looked at the bag in Garth's hand '– sugared nuts.'

Garth's eyes lit up. 'Is that where he lives? Is that where he keeps his slaves?'

Nicholas nodded and winced. 'It's most unusual for a European to be allowed inside.'

'The Count's a brute,' muttered Violet.

'Let's follow him and get him arrested,' cried Garth.

'Certainly not!' said Nicholas angrily. 'That would be far too dangerous. Besides, slavery is not strictly illegal here.' He paused and rubbed at a bead of sweat running down the side of his face. 'Look, I'd be grateful if you two would keep what we've seen to yourselves.'

Violet and Garth nodded and were silent. Nicholas Etherington was suddenly very serious indeed.

'Hurry now, *Violette!*' cried Madame, from behind them. 'We must return to the hotel for a rest before dinner!'

Violet spun around, suddenly furious at the sound of her governess's squeaky French voice.

'I don't *need* a rest before dinner!' she snapped. 'And I've barely had a chance to see the bazaar!'

As she spoke she stamped her foot, and the gold watch she wore around her neck swung upwards and glinted in the sun.

A second later, a tiny monkey leapt onto Violet's shoulders and wound its long, furry tail around her neck. To Garth's amazement, Violet didn't even jump. As Madame's face went purple with fury, Violet picked up the little monkey and held him in her arms.

Violet wondered if this was what was called love at first sight. The monkey was the size of a small toy teddy bear, with brown stripes down his cheeks and big, bright eyes. His fur was dark on his back and light on his stomach. Fixed into his ear was a small turquoise stud.

Madame let out a stream of rapid, shrieking French. *'Put that filthy beast down! You'll catch a disease! He's covered in bugs!'*

But Violet didn't even look up. The little monkey was holding on to her shiny watch and rubbing it against his cheek. In return, she tickled his ear.

'*Violette!*' screamed Madame backing away and waving her arms in the air. '*C'est horrible! Horrible!*'

A young boy who looked about the same age as Garth rushed up to Nicholas and spoke in rapid Arabic.

'What's he saying?' asked Garth, who had lost track of the conversation after the first word.

Nicholas laid a hand lightly on the Arab boy's shoulder to reassure him. 'This is Ahmed. He's a friend of mine. He says he is very sorry that the monkey jumped onto the pretty English girl.' Here Nicholas smiled at Violet. 'He is sure it was the brightness of her watch.'

'I don't care *what* it was!' screeched Madame. 'Take the little brute away!'

Violet ignored her governess. This was exactly the kind of stupid behaviour that made her more determined than ever to have her own way. 'What's the monkey's name?' she asked Nicholas.

'He doesn't have one,' replied Nicholas, after a few words with Ahmed. 'Ahmed says that the owner gives the monkey his name. That way they are friends for ever.'

'Ah.' Violet stroked the monkey's ear.

Madame grabbed Violet's hand. '*Non!*' she cried. '*Non! Non! Non!*'

'Don't pull at me so, Madame!' Violet jerked her hand away. Then she turned and gently gave the monkey back to Ahmed. 'Tell him I would call the monkey Homer if he was mine,' she said to Nicholas.

Nicholas translated. Ahmed flashed a white smile and spoke quickly in reply.

'He says he will call him Homer until you come back for him.'

Garth took one look at Madame's face and looked away, shaking with laughter.

# THREE

Violet sat between Garth and Nicholas Etherington and tried to pretend that she was drinking mint tea rather than the thin brown consommé she had been served in a large cup. Ever since she had been frogmarched back to the hotel by codfish to dress properly for dinner, Violet had been in a furious mood. It was so unfair that Garth should be allowed so much more freedom than she was. What was the point of wasting precious time having a maid fuss over your hair, when you could be looking at things you might never see again? Like the extraordinary sight of an Egyptian lady in a long white veil riding a donkey, whose shaved legs were painted with blue-and-yellow stripes. The lady had stared as Madame pulled Violet back to the hotel. Violet felt a wave of fury wash over her at the memory. She must have looked like a naughty child being taken home for a punishment.

Violet kicked at her chair-leg and felt her satin pumps rip on a wooden splinter. As the meal dragged on, she made it her business to shred the toes of both shoes.

'So, my dear,' said Lord Percy, kindly. He could see his daughter was feeling out of sorts. 'What would you like for Christmas?'

'Heavens, Percy,' cried Lady Eleanor. She dabbed her mouth with a snowy linen napkin and pushed away her plate of honey and apricots. 'What a question! Children like surprises!'

'I'm not a child, Mother,' said Violet angrily. 'As for what I should like for Christmas – I should like a monkey.' She pushed away her own untouched plate. 'And not just any monkey – I would like the little monkey in the bazaar with the turquoise stud in his ear.'

Lady Eleanor's dark almond-shaped eyes widened in her beautiful face. 'Good gracious, Violet. What an extraordinary request.' She smiled her lovely smile and twisted the emerald ring on her engagement finger. 'Absolutely out of the question, of course.'

'Of course, Mother,' replied Violet smoothly. 'But Papa asked me what I should like, rather than what I am likely to get.'

'Indeed, he did, my darling.' Lady Eleanor smiled and stood up. 'Shall we retire and leave the gentlemen in peace?'

As she stood up, she caught the eye of a large woman called Lady Wortley whom she had met when they first arrived. Her Ladyship was the size of a battleship, with a large shelf for a bosom and a face like a granite cliff. To match her looks, Lady Wortley had a loud, gravelly voice, and to everyone's distress – particularly Lord Percy's – an opinion on every conceivable subject. Her daughter, Henrietta, followed in her wake, as if invisibly drawn by some vacuum. Henrietta was a pale-faced girl with slightly protruding eyes and big teeth. She looked more like a nervous white pony than a young woman of seventeen. Violet had recognised her type immediately. She was the kind who preferred to sit about in the shade and read the social pages from out-of-date copies of *The Illustrated London News.*

Lady Eleanor had tried to encourage Violet to spend time with Henrietta instead of skulking about in the bazaar with Garth, but Violet had refused. It did not seem to occur to her mother, since she too liked lolling about reading magazines, that Violet might have other preferences.

Now Violet fought off an urge to grab the edge of the perfect damask tablecloth and tug it hard. Instead, she kissed her father on the cheek, thanked Nicholas for her expedition, and shot Garth a look that said *if you smirk, I'll murder you.* Then she pleaded tiredness and went to her room.

Garth didn't smirk. He could never understand the custom which dictated that the ladies leave the dinner-table while the men drank a glass or two of port and usually talked about business or gambling debts. And he sympathised wholeheartedly with Violet's views on Henrietta. He'd only managed five minutes with her before pretending he had a stomach ailment.

Garth looked across at Lord Percy. He was wearing an immaculate white bow-tie and a starched shirt-front. Nicholas was also dressed in formal evening clothes. That was another thing Garth couldn't understand. It seemed ridiculous to dress so elaborately when it was so hot. He wriggled inside his own stiff collar and fought off the urge to scratch his neck.

The waiter set down a decanter of port and three glasses. Garth watched as Lord Percy poured himself a small glass and passed the decanter to Nicholas on his left.

On the whole Garth didn't much like wine, but port was different. It was sweet. He tipped a little into his glass and watched as Lord Percy lit a thin, black cigar and sat back in his chair.

'What do you say we give Violet a surprise for Christmas?' he asked.

Nicholas sipped at his own port. 'If you are talking about the monkey, sir, we would have to go back to the bazaar immediately. Those little monkeys are very popular and it might have been sold by tomorrow.' He shrugged. 'If it hasn't gone already.'

Lord Percy leant back and sucked at his cigar. 'Who knows what Ahmed has done.' Garth saw a quick look pass between the two men. How did Lord Percy know about Ahmed? Suddenly he realised that Nicholas had told Lord Percy everything that had happened that afternoon. Garth forced himself not to stare at his friend but the question was huge in his mind: why?

'How long would it take you to change, young man?' Lord Percy paused. 'Garth!'

Garth almost knocked over his port. His thoughts were a million miles away. 'I'm sorry, sir. Five minutes, sir.'

'And you, Nicholas?'

'We'll stop at my lodgings on the way.'

'I hope you're in time.' Lord Percy held out a handful of coins. 'One more thing before you go, Garth. I have arranged a visit to the Great Pyramid for you and Violet at dawn tomorrow, before the sun is too hot. Madame will accompany you.'

A huge smile spread across Garth's face. He knew only too well how miserable Violet felt over dinner. Now she would have something to look forward to. 'Thank you, sir!' he cried. 'Does Violet know?'

'Madame was instructed to tell her after dinner.' Lord Percy smiled. 'I am hoping it will have improved her temper.'

Half an hour later, Garth walked with Nicholas Etherington through the torch-lit bazaar towards the square. In the light of the flames, the stall-holders' jewellery glittered like treasure.

'We'll be lucky if Ahmed still has the monkey,' muttered Nicholas, as they walked along the narrow alleyways.

Garth was amazed at how many people were still buying from the stalls. It seemed there was an endless supply of brooches, bracelets and necklaces. 'Don't people get angry if they find out they're buying fake antiques?' he asked.

'They don't find out, Garth.' Nicholas laughed. 'This is Egypt. What you don't know doesn't hurt you.'

'But there must be *real* scarabs,' said Garth. 'I've seen some in the British Museum. Do the market traders sell them too?'

'The market traders don't, but unscrupulous businessmen do.' Suddenly Nicholas's voice was serious. 'In fact, it's a big problem. These businessmen will stop at nothing to make their money. They hire robbers to ransack the tombs and then they smuggle the objects out of the country.'

'I thought tomb-robbers didn't exist any more!'

'They're worse now than ever because there's so much money to be made,' said Nicholas. 'What's more, they damage the tombs so that hundreds of smaller things are broken or lost. It's a filthy trade.'

As Nicholas was speaking, Garth suddenly saw Count Kapolski appear out of an alleyway. This time a woman in a heavy veil walked beside him, a young Arab following a few paces behind.

'Look, Nicholas!' he whispered. 'There's—'

A torch flared as the woman passed. Garth's heart lurched in his chest. He could see the outline of her face and it wasn't the face of Countess Maria. It was the lady he'd seen on deck with the Count just before they arrived in Alexandria.

Nicholas jerked Garth's arm and pulled him to one side, but at that moment the Count turned and stared straight at them. 'Blast!' muttered Nicholas. 'He's seen me.'

'What?' exclaimed Garth. 'Of course the Count's seen you! He was in the square this afternoon! He was on the steamer!'

'You don't understand,' said Nicholas. His voice was suddenly shaky. 'He never saw me on the steamer – that's why I travelled second class – and he didn't see me this afternoon.'

'What on earth is going on?' asked Garth. For the first time, he realised that Nicholas was frightened.

'Look,' replied Nicholas, as if he hadn't heard the question. 'You go over to Ahmed and tell him to keep the monkey for Violet.' He pointed to a shadowy doorway at the end of the street. 'I'll meet you in there. It's a tearoom.'

Garth stared at Nicholas's white, sweating face. He thought of the repulsive Count's pale eyes and thin smile. 'Why are you afraid of Count Kapolski?'

'Kapolski isn't his real name. It's Howard Dufort,' said Nicholas quickly. 'He's a notorious antiques smuggler and an extremely ruthless man.'

Garth opened his mouth to speak, but Nicholas held up a hand to stop him.

'Find Ahmed before he sells the monkey. I'll be in the tearoom.'

Garth was still awake at midnight. He hadn't been able to stop thinking about what Nicholas had told him. It turned out that Nicholas's father, Sir Edward, was not a businessman at all. He was the Curator of the Egyptian Antiquities Collection at a museum in London, and Nicholas had been working on a special mission for him to try to catch Count Kapolski red-handed. The problem was that the authorities didn't know how the Count managed to smuggle the objects out of the country so easily. It wasn't just happening in Egypt, Nicholas told Garth. The so-called Count also smuggled precious jewellery out of India. And now that the Count had recognised him, Nicholas said, the whole business was damned awkward. He'd already had one run-in with him in Cairo and the Count had sworn then that he wouldn't be let off so lightly again. When Garth asked what that meant, Nicholas had spread his hands. Half of the little finger on his left hand was missing.

Now Garth tossed and turned. He would never have guessed in a million years that Nicholas could be involved in something so dangerous. He looked like an old-fashioned student at a dusty university. Sometimes it was very difficult to understand English people. They were so good at pretending to do one thing and then doing another.

Garth stared out through the netting draped over his bed at the thin, new moon in a black, starry sky. He wondered whether he would ever learn to understand the grown-up world. Then he wondered if he would become just like the adults around him one day. It happened to everyone else. Why should he be any different? Garth sighed and curled up on his side. It wasn't as if he missed his home, because he'd never really had one. And as for his father, even though he'd felt close to him, he had seen very little of him over the past few years. In truth, Garth was happier now, with Violet, than he had ever been in America. He felt more at home with the English and Europeans than with his own people. Even so, sometimes everything became too confusing. Now that he knew there was danger as well, despite himself, Garth felt a little frightened.

A weary sleep overtook him.

# FOUR

Violet sat between Garth and Madame in stunned silence as the donkey trap rattled up the final sand-slope towards the rocky platform. A pale sun pushed upwards through pink-and-gold clouds. So far, the journey from the hotel had taken an hour and a half along a wide, busy road that had grown narrower and sandier as they drew nearer to the desert. And all the while, in the distance, the Great Pyramid rose in front of them.

At first the triangular shape was small and shadowy, and familiar from pictures Violet had seen in her history books. Then as they drew closer, it began to look more and more extraordinary. Finally, as the trap clattered up onto the platform, all three of them cried out. The Great Pyramid was so huge, it seemed to almost blot out the sky and the horizon beyond. It even seemed to blot out the sun. Nothing Violet had seen or read had prepared her for the sheer size of it.

'*Mon Dieu!*' whispered Madame. '*C'est énorme!*'

Garth leapt from the cart. 'Look, Violet!' he cried, pointing at a huge stone head set on top of a great rectangle of ridged stone. 'The Sphinx! The Sphinx!'

Violet jumped down beside him. Here was the creature she had tried to imagine all the way across the Mediterranean. A woman's head on a lion's body, half buried in sand. She fought back an urge to howl with delight.

'Come on!' cried Garth. 'Let's climb the pyramid!' He grinned at Violet. 'Last one to reach the top's a sissy!'

'I'm riding a camel first!' shouted Violet. 'First one to fall off's a *dolt*!'

'*Attendez! Attendez!*' cried Madame. But it was too late. Violet and Garth had set off along the rocky path with a guide who appeared out of nowhere, chattering and running beside them.

Madame watched as her two charges came to a row of camels. She saw Garth pointing at one and waving his hands, then Violet shaking her head and pointing at another. She smiled to herself and shrugged. They were right. Why *should* they wait? She wouldn't have at their age either.

Amelie Poisson hitched up her skirts, climbed down from the trap and set off after them.

'I'm getting on first,' insisted Violet, dodging to one side as the stinking camel in front of her, turned his great head and tried to spit in her face.

'Suits me,' said Garth. 'It was your idea.'

Violet clambered onto the small wooden saddle and held on to the bunch of sticky tassels tied to the front. The guide prodded the camel with his foot and the great animal rose, belching and shuddering, into the air. Violet went white. She had no idea camels were so big. She had been expecting something the size of a large horse. Now the ground seemed a very long way down. As the great beast moved forward, it swayed from side to side. For the first time since they left England, she felt seasick.

Beside her, Garth's face had turned green. 'I'm never listening to you again,' he shouted. 'I'm—' But she didn't hear anything else because the guide whacked his camel with a cane and it broke away at a trot.

The sight of Garth bumping up and down and yelling at the top of his voice made Violet howl with laughter, until her own camel lurched forward to keep up. Now it was *her* turn to be thrown about on a wooden saddle hard with sharp edges.

For the first time in her life, Violet was grateful for the layers of cotton camiknickers and petticoats Madame insisted she wear underneath her light cotton dresses. Even so, as the camel bounded forward, she felt herself beginning to lose her grip, and screamed.

'*Stop!*' Violet looked around to see her governess furiously thwack the camel boy with her parasol and point to their two camels. '*Stop!*' bawled Madame again.

The camel boy bellowed something in Arabic

and, to Violet's immense relief, the camel slowed to a stop. The next moment, it lurched forward onto its knees and she climbing, shaking, out of the saddle. Beside her, Garth did the same. The guide threw back his head and hooted with glee. Then he saw Madame's parasol twitching in her hands and the grin disappeared from his face.

'Wow!' muttered Garth, under his breath. 'Your codfish sure is scary when she means business.'

Madame took Violet by the hand. 'Enough of this camel-riding,' she said firmly. 'Now we climb the Great Pyramid.'

Four hours later, three Bedouin Arabs had pushed and pulled Madame up and over the mountain of sandstone blocks, and at last they had reached the top of the pyramid.

'You rest? Want drink?' An Arab dressed in baggy trousers and a shirt appeared with a goatskin full of water and a row of brass cups hanging from a pole that swung by his side. Behind him another man unrolled a dark-red awning and set it up over them.

Violet sat with Garth and looked out at the

endless desert behind and the distant, shimmering rooftops of Cairo in front. It was all so strange they might as well have been on the moon. The three of them gulped at the water and held out their mugs for more.

Violet was the first to speak. After the incident with the camels, she had decided to do everything properly. 'Would you come inside the pyramid with us, Madame? The paintings on the walls of the burial chambers are said to be very fresh still.'

Madame shook her head wearily. They still had to get all the way down again and she was exhausted. Yet she didn't want to deprive Violet of the chance to see inside a burial chamber. And doubtless her father would ask her about it later.

Garth turned and spoke to the guide. There was a rapid exchange of words, then the guide bowed and nodded. 'Yes please! Yankee doodle donkey!'

'What's he saying?' asked Violet, trying to keep the annoyance out of her voice. It really was unfair of Garth to pick up languages so quickly.

'He says he will take us down quickly and his brother will lead the esteemed Madame more slowly,' Garth grinned. 'That should give us time to visit the tomb and then meet up at his cousin's donkey stall, where there is some shade.'

The guide waved his hands and chattered.

'He wants you to know his cousin has many good donkeys for American and English tourists,' said Garth.

The guide whooped and hopped from foot to foot. 'Prince Wales donkey! Splendid! First rate! God save the Queen!'

Madame laughed and sat back under the shade of the red awning. 'Thank you, Garth! That is a most satisfactory arrangement. I will meet with you both in three hours.'

As it turned out, Garth and Violet were at the donkey stall well before Madame Poisson.

No sooner had Garth and Violet stepped into the stinking heat of the narrow corridor that led to the burial chamber than Violet's nostrils filled with a particular smell that made her stomach turn over. It was the sharp, pungent scent of geranium.

Violet thought she was going to be sick. Surely it

wasn't possible that the Count was in the tomb with them? But the smell was unmistakable. Underneath her cotton skirts, Violet's knees began to shake.

On their way down the pyramid, Garth had told her what had happened the previous night at the bazaar, only leaving out the arrangement he had made with Ahmed about the monkey.

In the dark, dusty corridor, Violet decided she wasn't taking any chances. She wasn't afraid for herself, but Garth could be in danger. If the Count was violent enough to cut off someone's finger, what would he do if he realised that Garth knew his real identity? There was nothing to stop him from putting a knife into his back in a shadowy corner of the burial chamber!

Violet grabbed Garth's sleeve, put a finger across his mouth and pulled him back into the sunlight.

'What did you do that for?' spluttered Garth, shaking her hand from his arm.

'The Count's in the tomb.' Violet's throat was so tight she could barely speak.

Garth stared at her. 'How do you know?'

'I smelt his hair oil. He was just in front of us.'

Garth chewed his lip and looked around for Madame. There was no sign of her. 'We'd better get out of here.'

He spoke to the donkey boy and explained they would wait for the French lady by the Sphinx's head. The boy nodded and led them to two donkeys.

'You should tell Nicholas,' said Violet, as they climbed onto the donkeys.

Garth nodded. 'I'll tell him tomorrow. He's joining us for the celebrations at lunch.'

Violet looked up. 'What's so special about lunch tomorrow?'

Garth rolled his eyes. 'It's Christmas Day, stupid!'

Violet scooped up another mouthful of the so-called Christmas pudding. She didn't like the kind they always ate in England. They were dark and heavy and sat like a lump of lead in her stomach. This one was completely different. It wasn't really a Christmas pudding at all. It was made with rice and almonds and cream, and seasoned with cinnamon and vanilla. She finished her plate and put down her fork.

'*Mish-mish*?' said the waiter behind her.

Garth translated. 'Apricots?' He helped himself. 'They really are quite delicious. Even better than the *totleh*.'

'That's the sweet jelly covered in almond slivers,' said Nicholas on her other side. He put down his fork, too. 'So, did you like your surprise present?'

Violet looked down at the exquisitely-carved cage on the floor by her side. The little monkey she had called Homer looked up at her with bright brown eyes. She picked up a piece of almond that lay on her plate and quickly pushed it through the narrow bars. The monkey took it in his delicate fingers and chewed it carefully.

'I don't think I've ever enjoyed a Christmas as much as this one,' she said, smiling.

Across the table, her father heard the joy in his daughter's voice. It was time for another surprise. He tapped the side of a crystal glass with his knife. 'Lady Eleanor has an announcement to make.'

Violet watched as her mother set aside her

napkin and stood up. It seemed that Egypt's extraordinary spell was even working on her. Lady Eleanor's face glowed with pleasure, and when she spoke her voice was as light and happy as a child's.

'I've found us the perfect boat!' she announced. 'It's called a *dehabiyah*. It's like a little Noah's Ark and it will take us up the Nile to Luxor!' She smiled around the table that shone silver-and-white and glittered with the reflection of candle-flames. 'We can travel in our own time and stop wherever we want to.'

'What's the boat's name?' asked Violet, excitedly.

'When do we leave?' cried Garth.

'It's called *Dongola* and we leave—' Lady Eleanor's eyes twinkled and she turned to Nicholas. 'That depends entirely on Nicholas.'

'What?' blurted Garth. He blushed scarlet. 'I mean, I beg your pardon?'

Nicholas was so taken aback he couldn't speak. He stared at Lord Percy, then back to Lady Eleanor, and appeared more and more confused.

'Papa!' said Violet firmly. 'I think you should explain yourself properly. It's not fair on Nicholas.'

'Quite right, my dear. It's very unfair.' Lord Percy smiled and looked at Nicholas. 'Lady Eleanor and I would be delighted if you could join us on our cruise down the Nile. What do you say?'

Violet watched as Nicholas's face flushed with pleasure. 'I would be truly honoured,' he said. He paused and turned to Lady Eleanor. 'I am ready to leave at any time. Indeed, any time that would suit you!'

'Excellent!' cried Lady Eleanor. To Violet's amazement she clapped her hands. 'We will leave at noon tomorrow. Everything will be ready for us then.'

Garth looked sideways as Nicholas took off his glasses and polished them with a napkin. Was it his imagination or did Nicholas look as if he had just won a reprieve? His hands were trembling and his forehead glistened with sweat, even as he struggled to keep his expression bright and excited.

Garth thought of Nicholas's missing little finger and shivered. Lady Eleanor's invitation had come at just the right time. With a man like Count Kapolski around, it would be a very good idea for Nicholas to be out of the way for a few weeks.

# FIVE

Violet stood with Madame on the crowded dock and stared at the boat that was to be her home for the next few weeks. Her mother was right. It looked just like Noah's Ark. The *Dongola* had two masts. There was a big one near the front of the boat and a smaller one at the back, behind a high cabin that looked like an open-air drawing room. From where she stood, Violet could see big cushions piled up along the walls and brightly-coloured rugs on the floor.

'Do you think we may look on board, Madame?' she asked, barely able to stop herself making the small jump from shore to deck.

Madame Poisson looked around. She tried to ignore the little monkey that sat quietly on Violet's shoulder. But even the thought of fleas and grubby paws could not ruin her mood. Amelie Poisson was entirely entranced by the boat – particularly since there was a piano in the dining saloon which she couldn't wait to try out.

Just at that moment, a wiry middle-aged man, dressed in striped baggy trousers and a black waistcoat, leapt out of the boat and stood beside them. He bowed low.

'Missy Winters, yes!' he cried. He spread his arms. 'Come! I show you!' He tickled Homer's ear and grinned. Then he bowed again. 'I am Hannan. I look after you!'

Violet smiled and bowed in return. She looked quickly at Madame who nodded, then she took the hand he offered and jumped onto the boat.

They worked their way down from the prow. The kitchen was just behind the big mast and, while it was barely more than a shed with a charcoal oven, a shelf and a row of saucepans, Violet was soon to discover that their cook, Reis, could produce endless delicious meals from there – even though the crew themselves ate only tea, lentils and dried bread.

Hannan led them through a doorway into the lower part of the boat. Here was a corridor with four sleeping rooms off it. Each one had a bed, a chair, a wash-stand and a looking-glass fixed to the wall. There was a row of hooks to hang clothes on and two big drawers under the bed. Violet tried not to think of Garth and Nicholas's plan to sleep on deck. While they would lie looking up at the stars, she would be stuck in a stuffy cabin looking up at the ceiling. With an effort, she pushed the thought from her mind. Nothing was going to ruin this morning.

Violet ran down the corridor and found herself in a long, wide room filled with sunshine, which poured in through four windows on each side and a skylight. The walls were panelled and painted white, edged with gold. A huge Turkish carpet was spread on the floor and there was a big dining-room table with a vase filled with flowers in the middle. Along one wall was an upright piano. Madame

71

immediately sat down and began to play a Chopin waltz. Violet could see that her father had already unpacked his guns and propped up his walking sticks in a corner.

Beyond the saloon was a double and a single sleeping room, and a bathroom. A narrow flight of steps led back to the upper deck. These cabins looked more comfortable than the others and there was more storage space. They would definitely be her parents' quarters. She left her dear codfish playing Chopin and climbed back onto the deck.

The wide, muddy river was filled with men rowing little boats in every direction. They dodged in and out of the sailing boats, reminding Violet of so many water beetles skittering over a pond. There was a constant babble of noisy, insistent voices. Violet pulled at the ties of her sun-hat. It was barely seven o'clock in the morning and already she could feel the heat prickling the back of her neck.

'Darling! Where's that useless French fish of yours? Really, what kind of—'

Lady Eleanor, dressed in pale turquoise and

apricot muslin, appeared like a phoenix rising from behind a mound of baggage.

'Madame is trying out the piano for you, Mama,' said Violet quickly. 'She particularly wanted to tune it for your trip.' She fixed her mother with an innocent look. Violet knew perfectly well that her mother resented the fact that she had not taken up with Henrietta Wortley, and had decided this was down to Madame Poisson's inadequate teaching. Lady Eleanor wasn't interested in education but she *did* have strong views on etiquette. Bad manners were inexcusable. Violet pursed her lips and tried not to look bad-tempered. She knew her mother had been working herself up into one of her furies and it would only be a matter of time before she suggested sending her codfish away.

'Really, Mama,' said Violet, in a coaxing voice. 'I do think you should be grateful to the French fish.' She laughed. 'Imagine five weeks of flat notes. It would be far worse than being bitten by a crocodile.'

But Lady Eleanor wasn't listening. 'I have asked Lady Wortley and Henrietta to join us,' she said smoothly. 'We will delay our departure by a day to give them time to prepare.'

Violet's jaw dropped. '*What!*'

'I beg your pardon,' said Lady Eleanor sharply.

'But, Mama!' protested Violet.

'No buts, Violet. Your deportment has been far from ladylike recently and I think Henrietta and her dear mother will be a good influence on you.' As she spoke she glared at Homer. 'And do remove that hairy little beast from your neck.'

Violet glared at her mother. Sometimes she hated her. 'Homer is not a hairy little beast,' she retorted. 'He's a Talapoin monkey and the only way he can be trained to obey is to be with me during the day.' She paused and played her trump card. 'Father agrees and gave his permission.'

Lady Eleanor pulled a face. 'What does your father know about monkeys? Besides, Lady Wortley informs me that Henrietta is allergic to animals.' With that, she turned and began to make arrangements with Hannan, who had been standing at a discreet distance.

Violet ran down to the saloon and explained to

Madame how she had left her cherished watch in her room and would Madame possibly go back with her to fetch it.

Ten minutes later, they sat in a donkey cart on their way to the hotel. Violet was fuming. On no account were Lady Wortley or her daughter coming anywhere near the boat. The trip they had all been looking forward to would turn into a disaster. She looked at her watch. It was almost ten o'clock. They were just in time to take morning tea with the Wortleys.

As the cart pulled up at the front of the hotel, Violet saw Garth standing on the pavement with Ahmed. Ahmed was talking rapidly and waving his hands in the air. Violet watched as Garth's face went from puzzled to pale. He reached into his pocket, handed over a coin, and ran back up the white stone steps.

Violet jumped out of the cart and followed him. 'Garth!' she cried. 'What's wrong?'

Garth stared at her. 'I've been looking for you everywhere!' His eyes slid sideways to the terrace, where Lady Wortley was moving between the tables like a wedding cake on stilts. Henrietta followed at her heels. 'I have to warn you—'

Violet followed his glance. 'The Wortleys? Don't worry. I'll take care of that.' She paused. 'What were you talking to Ahmed about?'

'Nicholas,' said Garth in a low voice. He looked around as if afraid someone might overhear him. 'Ahmed says he had an appointment to see him this morning and he never showed up.'

'Do you think the Count has something to do with it?'

'I don't know, but last night when your mother asked Nicholas to join us, he looked like a man who'd been thrown a life-jacket. There's no way he would change his mind and not let us know.'

Lady Wortley's ringing voice cut through the air like nails on a blackboard. Garth pulled a face. 'How are you going to fix them?'

'You don't want to know,' said Violet. 'Do me a favour and keep them talking. I have to get something from my room.'

'*Violette!*' cried Madame breathlessly. 'What on

earth made you jump from the cart like a jack-in-the-box?'

Violet shot Garth a glance and he moved smoothly to the French governess's side.

'Will you join me, Madame?' asked Garth, in his impeccable French. 'Violet and I were about to take tea with the Wortleys.'

'I'll just put Homer in his cage and fetch my watch,' said Violet. And, before her dear codfish could object, she ran across the great hall and up the stairs to her room.

Even though most of her luggage had been packed, Violet found what she was looking for quickly. The ipecac was in a small, brown, glass phial in her jewellery box. She had been reading about it before she left England. In small doses, it was most helpful for settling upset stomachs. In large doses, it made you quite ill – but only for a very short period of time and with no after-effects.

Lady Wortley was so busy lecturing Madame on the superiority of the English language that she didn't notice when Violet pretended to reach for the sugar, and instead put five drops of ipecac in her tea. As she had walked towards them, Violet had been trying to decide which one of them should get the dose. Then she had seen Henrietta talking to Garth. They were looking over the rails at a street magician. Away from her mother, Henrietta's face seemed to have something more than the look of a nervous horse. Violet had immediately made up her mind.

Violet was on the dock with her father when the note was delivered. It was from Lady Wortley. Regrettably she had to decline the Winters' kind invitation to sail up the Nile. She had fallen victim to a stomach disorder in the night and had been advised by the hotel physician to keep to her room for a few days.

Violet showed great disappointment at the news, even though she could not fail to notice how quickly Lord Percy pressed on with their arrangements. 'If only Nicholas Etherington would send word,' he muttered.

At that moment, a donkey cart rattled to a stop and Garth jumped down. He ran over to Lord Percy and handed him a letter. 'I beg your pardon, Lord Percy. It's a letter from Nicholas. Ahmed found me in the bazaar and asked me to give it to you immediately.'

Lord Percy broke the seal. His eyebrows knitted in a frown as he read the letter. 'Dear me,' he said. 'How unfortunate for young Etherington. He writes that he has just received a communication from his father and cannot leave Cairo after all. What a pity! I was looking forward to his company – he's said to be a damn good shot.'

The letter hung from Lord Percy's fingers.

Garth stepped forward. 'Shall I throw it away for you, sir?' he asked. His voice was flat. He had been looking forward to Nicholas's company, too.

'At least we know he hasn't been kidnapped,' said Violet, under her breath.

'I had better have a word with Lady Eleanor.' Lord Percy handed Garth the letter and laid a hand lightly on Violet's shoulder. 'I think we should leave as soon as possible.' A faint smile flickered across his face. 'We wouldn't want any miraculous recoveries, after all, would we?'

'Certainly not,' agreed Violet, wholeheartedly. She knew very well that her father's views on the Wortleys were not that different from her own.

'Good girl.' Lord Percy strode away across the busy quay, scattering small men carrying bundles on either side of him.

'Violet.' Garth's voice sounded strange and faraway.

Violet turned. His face was ashen. 'Whatever is the matter?' she asked in a worried voice.

'Nicholas didn't write this letter,' said Garth. 'I know his handwriting from when he was teaching me Arabic on the steamer. Whoever wrote this to your father presumed he wouldn't notice.'

A nasty, cold feeling passed over Violet even though the air was hot and sticky. 'You don't think . . .' but she couldn't finish her sentence. The idea that any harm had come to Nicholas was unbearable. She looked up and saw Garth staring over the river as if he was thinking hard. 'Something's going on and you're not telling me,' cried Violet angrily. She felt her eyes fill with tears.

The truth was that Garth was trying to fight a wave of panic that was making him feel faint.

'Don't be stupid!' he shouted, suddenly furious with her for not trusting him. 'We're in this together! I know as well as you do that that revolting Count is capable of anything.' He shouted at a donkey boy. 'I must see Ahmed. He's the only one who will know how to find Nicholas if he's being held against his will.'

Violet looked over to where her father was busy giving orders to Hannan. Even though she knew that nothing happened quickly in Egypt, Lord Percy usually got what he wanted. And he wanted to leave.

'Hurry!' she cried, as Garth climbed onto a donkey cart. 'Father is determined to go soon.'

# SIX

Hannan picked up his pistol and fired into the air. 'We go! Your Lordyships!' he shouted at the top of his voice.

Violet and Garth watched as the crew quickly loosened the mooring ropes and began to hoist the sail. Suddenly a woman's voice screamed high above the babble on the shore.

'Lady Eleanor! Help me! I beg of you!'

Everyone stared in astonishment.

Countess Maria Kapolski was running up and down the quay, waving at them desperately.

'Stop the boat!' bellowed Lord Percy.

'Not possibly, Lordyships!' cried Hannan. He pointed to the rapidly filling sail.

Violet heard the water gurgle past the hull as the boat surged into the main current of the river.

'Turn the damned thing round!' ordered Lord Percy.

'Yessir, Lordyship, sir!' Hannan spoke rapidly to his crew. He signalled to the young man at the tiller. The next moment, the boat turned and the sail flapped out on the other side. Now they were heading for the bank just as quickly as they had been moving into the middle of the river.

'What's she *doing* here?' cried Violet to Garth.

'Keep your voice down,' muttered Garth. 'How should I know?'

Garth felt miserable. Lord Percy had been ready to leave before he returned, and had been absolutely furious with him for going back into the city without permission. The only lame excuse Garth could manage to think of was that he had wanted to see the bazaar one last time. And that had only made Lord Percy more angry.

The truth was, Garth had looked for Ahmed everywhere but he hadn't been able to find him.

'*Mon Dieu!*' Madame hid her eyes behind her

hands as the boat moved through the water on what looked like a crash-course with the shore. 'What craziness is this?'

Violet watched as the figure of the Countess grew nearer. Now they could see she was surrounded by half a dozen pieces of luggage and a porter.

'Oh my goodness!' cried Lady Eleanor. She turned to her husband. 'Percy! It looks as if the Countess wishes to join us!' Her gloved hands flew to her mouth. 'What on earth shall we say?'

Violet saw her father push a look of deep irritation off his face. 'What *can* we say?' he snapped, still angry with Garth. 'We must welcome her aboard. I doubt she'll be travelling with us for long.'

'I don't know. I really don't know.' Lady Eleanor frowned. 'It is quite peculiar,' she said. 'I saw them get on the Luxor train with my own eyes.'

'Everyone's plans change, my dear,' said Lord Percy, suddenly seeing the look of abject despair on the Countess's face. 'I'd say there's been some spot of bother.'

The Countess looked as if she was about to collapse.

Garth turned to Violet. '*Something's* happened, that's for sure.'

Two hours later, the Countess was installed in the cabin that had previously been allocated to Nicholas and her baggage had been stowed as neatly as possible all over the boat. Even Lady Eleanor admitted there was an extraordinary amount of it. It was as if the Count and Countess had been planning a trip of months rather than weeks.

At last everything was in order and, after the Countess had rested, mint tea was served in the open-air drawing room on a round, low brass table.

'I'm so grateful for your kindness, my dear Lady Eleanor,' said the Countess in a husky, trembling voice. While her eyes were still tense, she seemed to have recovered some of her composure since she had stepped, shaking, onto the boat. 'I cannot think how the misunderstanding occurred. The Count's message was quite specific.' She shook her head and waved a finely-pleated paper fan in front of her face. 'He would not sail until I was able to join him.'

Lady Eleanor sipped her mint tea. All her instincts told her the Countess was not telling the truth, and she felt decidedly uncomfortable. 'I believed you were travelling to Luxor by train when I saw you last,' she said, lightly.

There was a silence. The two women looked at each other and the Countess's eyes dropped. Her new-found composure seemed to crumble and suddenly her pale face looked grey and sweaty.

'That was my understanding also,' she said, in a choked voice. 'Then he suddenly announced he had found a crew to take him up the Nile to shoot crocodiles, and all our plans changed.' She waved her fan again. 'He specifically told me he would not sail until I could join him.'

Lord Percy cleared his throat. 'I'd say we'll overtake the Count in a couple of days, my dear lady. He won't be going quickly if it's crocodiles he's after.' He held out his hand. 'In the meantime, we are honoured to have your company.'

On the deck, Violet and Garth heard every word. They had been lying in the shade, watching the men use a heavy bucket balanced over a frame to draw water out of the river.

'Just think,' said Violet. She half closed her eyes against the glare of the sun and ran a finger down Homer's back as he sat huddled happily on her shoulder. 'They've been using those buckets for thousands of years.'

'They're called *shadoufs*,' muttered Garth. He paused. 'She's lying, you know.'

Violet turned to make sure the codfish had not reappeared, but she shouldn't have worried. True to form, Madame had retired to the darkness of her cabin as soon as the boat had set sail.

'Not only that,' added Garth. 'I'm sure she doesn't live in Paris like she says.'

Violet's eyes widened. 'What makes you think that?'

'Because I overheard fish-face asking her where-abouts her house was, and she didn't even know the name of the district!' Garth frowned. The more he thought about it, the more he believed it was time to tell Lord Percy what they knew. Everything had changed since Nicholas had made them promise to keep what they had seen secret. Now Nicholas's own life could be in danger. 'I think we should tell your father about Nicholas. He'll know what to do.'

Violet shook her head. 'My father won't believe you. Worse than that, he might even tell the Count.' Then she remembered her father talking to Nicholas on the platform at Cairo station. She had been sure that they knew each other much better than each had pretended. She clenched her fists as she thought back over the steamer trip. Both of her parents appeared to be entirely taken in by the Count and Countess. How could they accept people who were so revolting? It didn't surprise her one little bit to discover now that the Countess was as much of a liar as her husband. The only strange thing was the Countess's distress at being left behind. Even though she may have lied about living in Paris, her distress seemed completely genuine.

'Garth,' Violet said, suddenly. 'I do believe the Count, or whatever he's called, abandoned his wife on purpose. I *don't* think she's lying about that.' She paused. 'And I think my father knows more about Nicholas than he's telling us. If we go to him now, he'll just treat us like naughty children. If we can find out a few more answers, he might take us seriously.'

Garth frowned. Violet was right. There was something going on between Lord Percy and Nicholas that neither of them knew about. 'Nothing explains why Nicholas didn't show up. For all we know he could be dead!'

'Garth!' cried Violet. 'Don't say that!' She almost stamped her foot. 'It's really not at all helpful!'

Garth looked up at her white, angry face. 'Sorry,' he muttered. He shook his head. 'It was stupid of me.'

'We'll have to sort it out ourselves,' said Violet firmly. 'Look. Let's put Nicholas's disappearance to one side for the moment. Why would the Count leave his wife behind on purpose?'

'For all we know, she isn't his wife in the first place,' said Garth. He shrugged. 'I never got the feeling they liked each other much.'

'Or he's changed sides and taken up with the woman in the veil?' Violet shuddered at the thought of the Count's face. 'Maybe she's more useful to him somehow.'

Garth shook his head again. 'Surely your parents wouldn't associate with such people?'

'It's impossible to say *who* they would associate with,' she said. 'Or why. What my father knows is one thing and what he tells my mother is something else.'

'I don't understand.'

It's hard to explain, thought Violet, ruefully. But she tried: 'Father knows all kinds of people – including people he isn't necessarily friends with. He has all kinds of arrangements.' She looked down and spread her fingers. 'I don't know what he does.'

Violet suddenly realised that she had never once asked Garth whether he had met her father in New York. He had crossed the Atlantic two or three times but never mentioned Garth or his father. The first time was when Conrad Hudson had died and he made the announcement that Garth was coming to live with them. It was strange.

'When you came to England, was that the first time you met my father?'

Garth was staring at a man on the shore leading a donkey so laden with bundles that it looked as if its bony knees would buckle at any moment. The question was so surprising, for a moment he couldn't think what Violet was talking about. 'Say that again.'

'Did you ever meet my father in New York?'

'No. Why do you ask?'

'He told me your father was one of his closest friends and that they often worked together.' Violet shrugged. 'I was just wondering.'

'They *did* work together,' said Garth. 'But it wasn't business – it was more to do with politics, I think. Anyway, all I remember is that when your father came to stay, everyone was sent to the country because his visit was supposed to be secret.'

Violet said nothing. It was always the same. As soon as she tried to get a clear picture of her father's life, she hit a dead end.

Garth looked back at the man and the donkey as the *Dongola* left them behind on the shore. Violet's question had jogged a memory he had forgotten. When he was six or seven, his father had come into the nursery and lifted Garth onto his lap. Garth remembered it well because his father hardly ever came up to see him. Especially at bedtime. They read a story about two men setting out on an expedition up a big river into the woods. They were looking for gold. Along the way one of them was attacked by a bear and the other saved his life by carrying him to an Indian camp where he was looked after.

'Why did he do that?' Garth remembered asking his father.

'Because they were best friends,' his father had explained. 'Best friends look after each other.'

Garth had thought about this for a moment. 'Do *you* have a best friend, Papa?'

His father had put down the book and ruffled his son's hair. 'I do,' he had said. 'His name is Lord Percy Winters. One day you will meet him.'

Violet watched Garth's face. 'What are you thinking?'

Garth told her. As he spoke, his face shrank and he looked sad and tired.

Violet touched his hand. 'I'm sorry. I shouldn't

have asked you. There's enough to worry about right now.'

'And I'm hungry.' Garth forced a smile back onto his face. 'I wonder when dinner is served on the Nile.'

Violet yawned. 'Late, I expect. When the heat dies down.'

They propped themselves up on some cushions and watched the reedy banks of the river drift past.

After a few moments, Violet spoke again. 'It's those dolphins, you know. The ones we saw as the *Lara* came into Alexandria.'

Garth snorted. 'You mean they've granted us our wish? We've got our mystery adventure?'

'Something like that.' Violet sat up on her elbows. 'And you know what?'

'What?'

'We're going to work it out all on our own.'

Garth sat up and, in true cowboy style, he shook Violet by the hand. 'Put it there, partner.'

That night they tied up on the river and, even though she was tired, Violet couldn't sleep. The heat in the cabin was stifling. She sat up and dragged her fingers through her itchy, sweaty hair. There must be a way to make herself cooler. She reached into a drawer under her bed and rummaged about until she found a fine cotton petticoat. It was lighter than the linen nightdress Madame had laid out for her. As Violet quickly changed, a puff of wind rocked the boat gently on its moorings.

Violet lay back down on her bunk and kicked off the cotton sheets. Through the window came the faraway barking of dogs and the croaking of hundreds of frogs in the reedbeds. She thought of Garth on the deck, and felt even hotter and itchier. She knew she would never be allowed to sleep out, but why should Garth have all the fun? Violet decided to ask her father to teach her to shoot next time he went out with Garth to hunt sand-grouse. It was only fair. A plan quickly took shape in her mind. For each lesson he gave her, she would paint him a watercolour. She knew he loved her paintings.

Violet smiled in the darkness. Her sudden dedication to her easel would also help keep her mother off her back.

# SEVEN

A week passed by and there was no sign of the Count or, indeed, any crocodiles. Violet and Garth took it in turns to watch out for a pair of unblinking yellow eyes floating on the water or something that looked like a rotten log. But they saw nothing. Instead, there were pelicans with enormous yellow bills and paddy-birds that rose in their hundreds from the reeds.

'I bet the Count has pushed on towards Luxor,' said Garth, one afternoon, as he peered through a pair of field-glasses at a row of vultures. They looked like tiny monks, with their hooded eyes and rounded shoulders. 'Hannan says that so many crocodiles have been killed on this stretch of river, you have to go further now. By the way . . .' He put down the field-glasses. 'Have you noticed that neither your father or mother have mentioned Nicholas's name since the Countess came on board?'

Violet nodded and stroked Homer's ears. The little monkey chirruped and tucked himself closer into the curve of her neck. Violet had become so fond of him, she could hardly imagine a time when he hadn't been with her.

'It makes me think they know more than they're letting on.' She took the glasses and stared at the vultures herself. 'Even so, I say we should wait until we catch up with the Count before saying anything to Father.' She ran her tongue over her lips. They were still sticky from the glass of fizzy lemonade she'd drunk at lunch-time. 'It can't be long now.'

At that moment, the codfish appeared on deck with a notebook in her hand. She made her way unsteadily towards them. Though the water was almost flat and she had been on the boat for over ten days, Madame still walked as if she was about to fall over.

'Birds,' muttered Violet.

'What?'

'She's going to ask us about birds. It's our lesson for today.'

Garth stood up as Madame settled herself on a large, embroidered cushion.

'Good afternoon, Madame,' he said, bowing. 'Do you think vultures prefer rotten fish, rotten goat or rotten lamb?'

Madame arranged her hat to hide a smile. If he was trying to make her feel sick, it hadn't worked. 'Rotten lamb, most certainly, *mon cher* Garth. But perhaps, if they are very hungry, they will not be so fussy in their eating habits.' She paused. 'Unlike some American gentlemen of my acquaintance.'

Garth grinned. He had grown quite fond of Madame Poisson. Despite her so-called 'delicate constitution', she had become the nurse on-board, cleaning minor cuts and soothing sun-strained eyes with her diluted rosewater potions. Of course, right now, Garth knew she was referring to his refusal to eat his lunch.

'I'm sorry, Madame,' he said, grinning. 'I can't eat lentils and buffalo cream.'

'Can't or won't?' replied Madame.

'Won't,' said Violet, taking the chance to score a point. '*I* eat them, Garth, *and* that *sorghum* stuff. She pulled out a sketchbook and showed her governess a painting of a kingfisher. 'Do you like it?'

Madame looked at the flash of bright-blue feathers against the silver-green of the reeds. 'Very well done, *Violette*,' she said. 'Your mother will be pleased and your father obliged to lend you a gun once again.'

Violet grinned. Her dear codfish had understood the thinking behind her plan the moment she had proposed it. Now Madame rearranged her navy-blue skirts on the cushion to make herself more comfortable.

'However, I did not come to talk about birds. Your mother is suggesting an expedition this afternoon. We tie up at a town called Minieh. Would you like to walk and sketch with your mother and the Countess?'

There was silence while Violet tried to guess whether there was an alternative or whether, if she said no, she would have to stay on the boat. 'Is there another party?' she asked finally.

'Yes. Hannan is going to the market.'

Violet's eyes brightened. 'May I go with him? I would be quite happy to buy anything you need.' Her voice tailed off hopefully.

'That is very kind of you, *Violette*, but unnecessary, as I would also prefer to go to the market.'

'May I join you both?'

'My dear Garth! We would be delighted.' Madame beamed at the young man she was growing increasingly fond of. 'Indeed, I was quite depending on your services as a translator!'

Three hours later, after a long walk along a narrow path through sandy scrub, Hannan led the party of four – Homer had been allowed to join them at the last moment – to a tiny town of mud huts and dusty alleyways. The market was spread out in the widest of the alleys, which was covered with a roof of rotten matting. As in Cairo, the merchants sat cross-legged in front of stalls no bigger than cupboards, but Violet noticed that the saddles, rugs and jewellery they were selling here were dirty and badly made.

Violet tried not to return the stares of the country people who sat on the ground behind their baskets of fruit and vegetables and eggs. Boys leading laden donkeys and women swinging squawking bundles of chickens pushed their way through the crowded alley. Sometimes the clouds of flies were so thick Violet had to hold her breath as she walked through them, for fear they would fill her nose and mouth.

A woman squatting behind a mountain of eggs screamed something at Garth, but he shook his head. Beside her, an old man shook a vast wicker cage full of pigeons and yelled insistently. Again, Garth shook his head.

'What was that woman saying?' asked Madame.

Garth laughed. 'She wanted me to buy a hundred eggs for fourteen pence. And the old man says pigeons are a bargain at thruppence a brace.'

'Father likes pigeon,' said Violet. 'Shall we—'

'*No*,' said Madame firmly. 'That is Hannan's job. He would be very upset if you thought he wasn't doing it well.'

Garth turned and saw a flaking metal sign hung

over a door. A picture of a tin of Bovril swung above it. 'There's the shop Hannan told me about,' he said excitedly. 'We'll find everything we need here!'

A moment later, Garth held aside the beaded curtains and Violet and Madame stepped into a low, dark room that stank of castor oil and lentil soup.

Violet couldn't believe her eyes. Behind the tubs of dates and sugarcanes and piles of limes and cabbages, there was a shelf of bottled English beer, French claret and Worcester sauce. Below them were stacks of tea biscuits, tins of sardines and preserved meat, pots of marmalade and even bars of Pears soap. She turned to Garth, who was standing at the side of the shop, near where two men were leaning against the counter, smoking pipes and gossiping.

Madame Poisson was peering at a shelf of Beecham's Powders, Garston's Cordial, Eno's Fruit Salts and Virol Malt. Violet walked over to join her and shuddered. She hadn't seen medicines like these for weeks and she never wanted to see them again. She pulled at her codfish's arm before she got it into her head to buy some of them. 'Have you found your writing paper, Madame?'

'Not yet. I have looked everywhere, but perhaps Garth will ask for me.' Her eye caught a pile of matchboxes. 'Ah, yes, that reminds me. I heard your father mention he was running out of cigars.'

Violet watched as Garth picked up a small, yellow melon and pretended to smell it. She could see he was listening to the two men, who were still talking.

Madame patted him on the shoulder. 'I would like some cigars, please, Garth,' she asked quickly. 'For Lord Percy, of course!'

'We have not cigars, madam,' said the greasy-looking man in English. He shrugged and stared rudely at her. 'Come back tomorrow.'

'Do you have writing paper?' asked Madame Poisson, in a slightly sharp voice.

'Naturally.'

Garth threw Violet a look that said he had something important to tell her.

'May I wait outside, please, Madame?' She pretended to feel faint. 'The air is fresher there.'

'Of course.'

Garth followed her out. 'The Count was here yesterday,' he said quickly. 'He paid that man not to mention it to any foreigners.'

Before he could say any more, Madame walked stiffly out of the shop with a box of writing paper and two bottles of ink wrapped in brown paper.

'What a filthy ogre of a man,' she said, her face red with fury. 'I shall speak to Hannan about him.' She grabbed Violet's arm as if to protect her from some unseen threat. 'Come along – we're going back to the boat.'

Violet never saw the eagle that swooped over her head, its hungry, yellow eyes fixed on Homer's small body. She only heard the monkey scream with terror. The next thing she knew, he was running into the bush.

Ahead of her, Garth was walking with Madame. The two of them were talking rapidly in French. It always amazed Violet how the codfish seemed to come alive when she spoke her own language. She seemed to have forgotten the nasty man in the shop, and was laughing with Garth as she pointed to a circle of palm trees and tethered camels about half a mile ahead of them.

Violet called out, but neither of them heard her. Meanwhile Homer was about to disappear into a field of *sorghum*. Violet turned off the path and ran over the rocky sand towards him.

The next thing she knew she was falling down a steep shaft into the desert.

At first, Violet was too surprised to be frightened. She had landed on soft sand with no broken bones. And, to her great relief, Homer jumped onto her lap from the darkness. 'You silly creature!' she scolded him. 'Now, come along, let's go and catch up with the others.'

It was only when she looked up and saw the small circle of sunlight at the top of the shaft that she realised the situation she was in. Only the night before, her father had been talking about the dangers of concealed tomb shafts in the desert. As the tombs themselves were often robbed, the entrances to the burial chambers were left unmarked. Sometimes sandstorms revealed shafts that had been hidden for thousands of years. And sometimes people fell down them and were never seen again.

As Violet sat in the dark, gritty hole, she tried to force down the panic that was surging through her. It was hot and the tunnel in front of her was probably full of snakes and scorpions. She bit back a scream and huddled against the wall. At least it seemed reasonably firm.

As she shifted in the sand, Violet felt something hard prod her bottom through the cotton of her petticoats. She reached into the sand and her fingers felt the outline of a brooch. She held it up to the light coming through from the top of the shaft. She was holding a pendant carved in the shape of an eye, surrounded on either side by carvings of a cobra and a vulture. The vulture reminded her of the eagle that had frightened Homer. And, suddenly, she knew what to do.

Violet ripped a length of satin ribbon from her petticoat and tied it around Homer's neck. Then she stood on her tiptoes and pushed him out into the daylight.

'Find Garth,' she whispered, her voice catching in her throat. 'Bring him here.'

For a moment, Homer clung onto her wrist. 'Go,' sobbed Violet. 'Go! You're my only hope!'

# EIGHT

Violet sat down in the tunnel she now knew would be her tomb if Homer did not come back. With a sinking heart, she stared up at the circle of light as the blazing blue sky turned from pink to gold and suddenly to black. The pendant was heavy in her hand and somehow it was comforting to polish it again and again with the hem of her skirt. In a crazy way, she started to hope it might be some kind of Aladdin's lamp. Even if a genie didn't appear in front of her, she might get granted a wish.

Violet wiped the tears that were filling her eyes and wished desperately that she would not be left to die here, buried alive in the desert. Despite herself, tears began to drip down her cheeks. She realised that she was incredibly thirsty, and felt for the flat, leather water-bottle her father had insisted she carry with her whenever she left the boat. It was half full. She pulled out the cork and sipped the warm, musty water. It tasted sweet and delicious. She gulped the whole lot, before realising how stupid that was. She put back the cork after a couple of sips. By now she was sitting in complete darkness and, for the first time, felt cool air settle around her. She moved to one side so she was not directly beneath the hole, then leant back against the wall and tied the pendant around her neck.

Perhaps it would bring her luck.

At first Violet thought she was imagining the voices, and had to force herself not to cry out. They were coming from the end of the tunnel in front of her. Violet sat dead still and concentrated as hard as she could. Over the muffled sounds, one voice rang louder than the others. Her blood ran cold. It was a voice she had hoped never to hear again.

Count Kapolski.

'*Dépêche-toi, idiot!*'

Another man replied in French. His voice sounded sullen. Then the Count spoke again. This time he sounded as if he was swearing. There was a shattering *crash*, as if something like pottery was being thrown against stone.

Violet shrank against the wall and cursed herself for not paying attention during her French lesson with the codfish. She could sense the men were arguing, but they were speaking so fast it was almost impossible to make out what they were saying. She strained to understand what she could. Three words were mentioned over and over again: *gold, crocodile, star.* Then, to her horror, she heard the Count mention her parents' names. He laughed unpleasantly. The other men snorted, as if in agreement. Tears began to trickle down Violet's face again. As she tried desperately not to sob, she became aware that there was some kind of rhythm to the noise the men made. There was a dragging sound, as if heavy objects were being moved from one place to another, then a bang, as if something

111

was being dropped into a crate. There was the sound of hammering. Then it stopped.

'*Allons-y!*' said the Count. *Let's go!*

Violet felt sick. One terrible thought filled her head. This could be her last chance to get out of the tunnel alive. Violet held her head in her hands to stop herself shaking. She knew she didn't have a choice. It was madness to stay where she was. Expecting Homer to bring Garth back had been crazy. Apart from anything else, the little monkey had only been with her for two weeks. It would be a miracle if Homer had run anywhere except straight into the bush. Violet raised herself onto her hands and knees and looked up at the circle of stars at the top of the shaft. Then she began to crawl towards the Count.

At that moment, two things happened.

Homer landed on her back and Garth jumped down beside her with a lantern in his hand.

As quickly as she could, Violet pointed along the tunnel and then at the lamp, drawing her finger across her throat with her other hand. Garth doused the light.

'What's that damned racket?' snarled the Count, in the darkness ahead of them.

For the first time, Violet heard a woman's voice. She spoke smoothly in French and seemed to be asking a question.

The Count snapped out a reply.

A moment later, there was silence.

In the light of the moon, Violet watched in horror as Homer scampered off down the tunnel. She turned to Garth. His face was drawn and she saw her own fear reflected in his eyes. He reached out and patted her shoulder. Both of them knew it was too dangerous to talk.

Two minutes later, Homer scampered back again and jumped onto Violet's shoulder. He wrapped his small, skinny arms around her neck and nuzzled her ear. Violet leant over to Garth. 'I think it's safe.'

For a moment, Garth hesitated. Was he being completely mad to put his faith in a monkey? Then he remembered how Homer had leapt aboard the *Dongola*, screeching and pulling at his clothes. Garth nodded and the two of them started to crawl down the tunnel on their hands and knees. If the Count had gone, there must be a way out.

After a few hundred yards, the walls of the tunnel widened so that they couldn't feel them on either side. Violet's heart pounded in her chest. For all she knew, she was crawling along a spit with an abyss dropping away on either side. At last she could bear it no longer. She reached out and grabbed Garth's ankles. 'I can't go on.'

It was the first time she had spoken out loud since she fell down the hole. Garth stopped and they sat down in the dirt.

'Have you got any water?'

Violet shook her head. 'I finished it all.' She felt a heavy flask of water being pushed into her hands.

'Drink it,' said Garth, in an urgent voice. 'Your parents are looking for you everywhere. We don't have a lot of time before we're found out.'

As Violet drank, she felt her mind clear. 'Are they blaming the poor codfish?'

'They don't have to,' replied Garth. 'Your poor codfish is blaming herself.' He took back the flask and fitted it into the leather case that hung from his belt. 'Now, quickly, did you hear the Count say anything that might help us?'

Violet racked her brains for all the words she could remember, but there were still no more than three.

'Gold, crocodiles, star,' Garth muttered, when she had finished speaking. 'Search me.' He untied the lantern from his belt. 'I think it's safe to light this now.'

Violet thought of the abyss she had imagined on either side. 'Yes, let's.'

Garth struck a match. A second later, the lantern threw out a bright circle of flickering light. To their amazement, they discovered they were in a room like an enormous bread oven. The walls were painted with animals and birds, and the colours and shapes were as bright and sharp-edged as if they had been painted the day before. On one side of the room were two wooden boxes. A hammer lay on the ground beside them.

For a moment, Violet and Garth could only stare around them.

'Hold the lantern,' said Garth, as if breaking a

spell. 'We have to find out what the Count was doing.'

He picked up the hammer and prised open a box.

Inside were lots of odd-shaped bundles of sacking cloth. Garth lifted one up. It was about the size of a man's shoe and heavier than he'd expected. He laid it carefully on the sand.

Violet held up the lantern as Garth pulled back the cloth. Inside was an exquisitely-carved ebony panther. The ears and nose were inlaid with gold and the eyes were made of polished green quartz.

It was the most beautiful thing either of them had ever seen. Violet turned back to the other two boxes. If they were both full of objects like this, they would be worth hundreds of thousands of pounds.

Garth wrapped up the panther and put it back in the box. Then he nailed the lid down. No one would ever know it had been opened.

'It's just as Nicholas said,' muttered Garth. 'The Count's a tomb-robber.' He tried to lift the box. It was incredibly heavy. 'But how does he smuggle the artifacts out of the country? I mean, there must be hundreds of them – and this is only one tomb.'

Suddenly Violet felt as if she was going to burst into tears. If only she hadn't been so lazy with her French, she might have been able to tell Garth the answer. They might even have been able to find Nicholas.

Garth looked across at her. 'Come on,' he said gruffly. 'I've been stupid. I should have taken you straight home.'

Violet nodded but said nothing. She knew that if she spoke her voice would crack. To make things worse, the lucky pendant she had found in the sand had gone from her neck. It must have fallen off as they crawled through the tunnel.

Garth held up the lantern. There were footprints all over the gritty sand. They followed them along a corridor into another oven-shaped room. Except this one was empty.

On the far side of the room, a wooden ladder led up to a trap-door.

'What shall we do if it's locked?' whispered Violet nervously.

'We'll worry about that later.' Garth climbed the ladder and shoved at the trap-door with his shoulder. It wasn't locked and opened creakily onto a cool star-lit sky.

Garth held up the door and pulled Violet out into the night. At that moment, Homer scrambled up the ladder and jumped onto her shoulder. Something hard and cool swung around and hit her on the neck.

It was the pendant.

'What's *that*?' asked Garth, as he let the trap-door down and covered it over with sand.

Violet laid it in his hand. 'I don't know, but it saved me.'

Garth stared at the turquoise eye in the centre of the pendant. It seemed to look back up at him. A strange feeling crawled over his skin. It was as if he could *feel* the ancient power in the jewel. But it was a sympathetic power, not a terrifying one. He handed it back to Violet. 'Funny,' he said slowly. 'I think you're right.'

They looked around them. It was dark except for the light of a half-moon, and all they could make out were dark clumps of bushes and a scattering of boulders.

'We'll never be able to find this place again,' said Violet. She stroked Homer's furry head as he curled against her ear.

Garth pointed up to the sky. 'Yes, we will. There's the Plough and that's the North Star just beneath.' He pulled out a compass and squinted at it in the lantern-light. 'If we walk north and then west, we'll come to the river. Then all we have to do is follow it down to where the boat is and retrace our steps.'

Violet stared at him. 'How do know all this?'

'I'm an American!' Garth grinned at her. 'Want to hear another of my camping stories?'

The moon was high in the sky when they finally saw the *Dongola,* rocking gently at her mooring. Garth shouted to Hannan, who was sitting hunched up on the prow, staring anxiously at the bank.

Within ten minutes, Violet was installed in a warm bath and Homer had been awarded the freedom of the boat.

To Violet's surprise, neither of her parents was

angry with her for chasing after Homer. They were both far too relieved to have her back safe and sound. Apparently Lord Percy had been in the town organising a search party when Homer returned to the boat, so Garth had followed the monkey on his own. As for Madame, every time she saw Violet, she burst into tears and threw her arms around her. Once she even managed to tickle Homer's ears.

All the next day Violet was treated like an invalid. She had to rest on a pile of cushions under an awning on deck and anything she wanted was brought to her. Strangely, Violet found that after the terrors of the dark tunnel she was extraordinarily tired, so she was quite happy to lie quietly while Madame read to her or sat beside her and mended the tears in her petticoats.

That night, Lord Percy fired the gun twice to officially celebrate Violet's safe return. Reis had cooked a special dinner of fish fillets with spices followed by lamb kebabs and peppers stuffed with rice. When the table was finally cleared and the fruit was taken away, Lord Percy sat back in his chair.

'So, my dear girl. Now that you're rested, will you tell us exactly what happened?'

Violet exchanged a quick look with Garth. They had decided on a strategy on their way back to the boat.

With her eyes on the Countess's face, Violet reached into the little purse she wore at her waist and took out the pendant. Madame had cleaned and polished it so now the jewel sparkled more brightly than ever.

'I fell down a tomb shaft,' Violet said simply. 'I found this in the sand.'

It was immediately clear to everyone that the pendant was incredibly old and valuable, but it was the Countess's reaction that Violet and Garth were interested in. And they were surprised at what they saw. Instead of gasping or looking guilty or frightened, the Countess's face went very solemn. She held out her hand and took the pendant from Violet's fingers.

Lady Eleanor watched as her guest stared at the jewel for a long time before speaking. 'Dear me, Countess,' she said at last, when the silence had become almost embarrassing. 'I had quite forgotten you told me on the steamer that you were something of an expert in Egyptian jewellery.'

The Countess looked up with her black, serious eyes. 'I'm only an amateur, Lady Eleanor. However, this is a very special pendant.' She laid it down on the tablecloth. The turquoise stone shone even brighter against the white damask. 'This is the healing eye of Horus,' she said in a voice barely louder than a whisper. The vulture symbolises the goddess Nekhbet and the snake is the goddess Wadjet.'

She fixed her black eyes on Violet, but they were so dark that they were almost expressionless. 'The pendant gives the wearer powerful protection,' she said.

The Countess handed the jewel back to Violet. 'You have been very lucky. Who knows what might have happened?'

Throughout their conversation, Garth had been watching Lord Percy. He could see from the look on his guardian's face that Lord Percy had been observing the Countess's reaction to the pendant as closely as he and Violet. Once again Garth asked himself how much Lord Percy knew about what was going on. And he wondered whether he ought to tell him what he and Violet had discovered. Then again, Garth understood that Lord Percy was quite capable of demanding the truth if he wanted to hear it. Perhaps Violet was right. They would only be branded 'naughty children' if they went to him too early with what they had found out.

Lady Eleanor gasped as she listened and her beautiful white hands fluttered to her mouth. 'My dear Countess!' she cried. 'Are you saying Violet could have been buried for ever?'

'Please,' murmured the Countess. 'Don't upset yourself, Lady Eleanor. I would merely suggest that the young people are more circumspect about their wanderings in the future.'

'Indeed,' murmured Sir Percy. 'Heaven knows what might have happened to them.'

Violet didn't dare look at Garth.

That night the wind got up and screamed around the boat. By the time morning came, the water was grey and choppy and the shore almost invisible in swirling sand.

Everyone on the boat was edgy. No one said it aloud but they were all thinking that if the storm had come one day earlier, Violet would never have been found alive. Lady Eleanor and the Countess kept themselves to their cabins while Madame huddled in a corner, trying to write letters. But the sand got in everywhere and the ink bottle was full of grit.

'*Mon Dieu!*' Madame cried in exasperation as she shook out her pen and covered the page in blots of ink. She scrumpled up the paper and, without another word to either Garth or Violet, stomped out of the room.

Even Hannan, whose dark face was usually covered in smiles, stalked about the boat, snapping at his crew.

'*Hamsin!* Sandstorm!' he shouted at Garth over the screech of the wind, waving the boy back inside. Bad things happened during sandstorms. Hannan prayed to the gods that it would soon blow over.

Back in the saloon, Garth put down his copy of

*Sherlock Holmes* and looked over to where Violet was trying to paint a picture of the carved panther they had seen in the vaulted room. The windows along either side of the room were covered in fine sand. On deck it was as if a camel-hair blanket had been laid over the boards.

'You *were* lucky,' said Garth, quietly. 'I'd never have found you in this storm.'

Violet touched the pendant that hung around her neck. 'I'm praying for Nicholas. Let's hope this is powerful enough to find him, too.'

Garth got up and kicked at the cushions. He was as cross and irritable as everyone else. 'We won't find Nicholas until we catch up with that crook who calls himself a Count.' He glared at the pendant around Violet's neck. 'And none of that mumbo jumbo is going to make any difference.'

At that moment, Lord Percy walked into the room. He had obviously heard what Garth had said, but made no comment. He crossed to where Violet was painting.

'How extraordinary,' he murmured. 'I've just been reading about panthers.'

'This one was carved out of ebony,' said Violet, in an even voice.

'How extraordinary,' said her father.

Again it was on the tip of Garth's tongue to tell Lord Percy everything they knew. Then he caught Violet's eye. She stared at him hard. She had given her father a chance and he hadn't taken it. And that could only mean that he didn't want them involved. It would be useless to appeal to him. They were on their own.

As Lord Percy left the room, Garth threw himself back down on the cushions and opened his book. To his fury, he discovered he had lost his place.

# NINE

The storm lasted for a day and, by the end of it,
every single crack in the boat had a fine coating of
yellow dust. Everyone's hair was matted with sand.
Their mouths were dry and their eyes were sore and
prickly. All the books and papers, carpets and
cushions were covered, no matter how many times
the servants came to sweep the sand away. That day
nobody bothered to eat. The idea of gritty food was
unbearable. Then, just as Lady Eleanor was about to
vent her rage on Madame who, for some reason, she
held responsible for the sandstorm, thunder crashed
overhead. A moment later, the noise of drumming
rain on the cabin roof made it impossible to speak.

Without asking anyone's permission, Violet and Garth ran out on the deck. They had been arguing all morning. Despite Lord Percy's aloofness, Garth still believed they should tell him what they had seen and heard in the tomb. They owed it to Nicholas. Garth accused Violet of putting her own sense of self-importance above her concern for Nicholas's safety. Violet retorted that it was precisely her fear for Nicholas's safety that made her want to wait a little longer.

'We've got this far without them, Garth! Don't you see, they're grown-ups. They do things by the rules. No matter what you think, they still believe we're children and they know best. The Count isn't expecting us to know about him. It's our biggest advantage.'

'Oh, shut up!' Garth had snapped.

'No! You shut up!' Violet had shouted.

Now, as the warm water soaked their clothes and washed the dust from their hair, their anger disappeared They tipped a canvas bucket of water over each other's heads and burst out laughing.

*

At lunch that day, everyone had extra-big helpings. Even Lady Eleanor admitted to feeling hungry after refusing to eat during the sandstorm. Violet had just swallowed a mouthful of rice cream when there was a sharp *crack* of rifle-fire outside.

Across the table, the Countess jerked in her chair. She put down her spoon with a trembling hand.

Violet tried to look as if she hadn't noticed, but the spoon rattled against the china bowl with a noise that seemed to be almost as loud as the gunfire.

'Heavens,' cried Lady Eleanor. 'That sounds like a gun going off!'

'It is, my dear,' said Lord Percy, calmly. He turned to the Countess. 'I'd say we have finally found your husband.'

'May I get down from the table, Papa?' asked Violet.

'Certainly,' replied her father. He looked across the table. 'I'm sure Garth will be happy to accompany you on deck.'

'Thank you, sir,' muttered Garth, desperately trying to cram in one more mouthful of rice cream before the table was cleared. It was all very well for the ladies to stop eating, but after yesterday's abstinence Garth was starving. He had even sneaked down to the crew's quarters in the night to ask for some of their lentil soup and bread.

On deck, Violet stared at the *dehabiyah* tied up a few hundred feet ahead of them, a look of revulsion on her face. Hanging from the hull, like teeth on a terrible necklace, were the bodies of six Nile crocodiles. Beyond the boat, on the flat riverbank, two turbanned men were dragging something that looked like a rotten log over the greasy, black mud. Further on, the bodies of three more crocodiles had been hauled high up the bank and were lying on flat, dry stones. A man was bent over one of them. The silver blade of a curved knife glinted in the sun.

Beside her, Garth peered through a pair of field-glasses. 'It's that Arab from the bazaar in Cairo,' he said.

'What Arab?'

'The one I saw following the Count after he came out of the merchant's house.'

Violet looked through her own field-glasses. She

watched in horrified fascination as the Arab plunged the curved knife into the crocodile's belly and expertly made a cut from one end to the other. Within moments, he had removed the crocodile's insides and tossed them into the middle of a flock of squawking birds a few feet away. Although her stomach was heaving, Violet looked back at the other crocodile carcasses that had already been gutted. Their skin was peeled back and neatly pegged to the ground and they had been filled with something that looked like salt.

Suddenly Garth reached out and pulled her field-glasses away from her face.

'The Count's coming! He'll see the glint of the glasses!'

Violet crouched behind the stubby mast. She watched as the Count and two other men pushed aside the reeds and walked onto the beach. It was clear that they hadn't yet noticed the arrival of the Winters' boat. The Count walked over to the dead crocodiles and prodded them with his boot. The Arab pointed to the white grit in the animal's gut and made a gesture with his hands. The wind carried the sound of the Count's voice away over the water. He prodded the crocodile again and the Arab nodded and went on with his work.

'Do you think that Arab is the Count's slave?' whispered Violet. She shuddered at the mere thought of it.

'I shouldn't think so,' said Garth. 'By the look of him, he's some kind of taxidermist.'

Violet nodded. The man did seem to know exactly what he was doing.

They both watched in silence as the Arab quickly pegged back the wide flaps of skin.

'Then maybe he's—' Garth didn't finish his sentence because, at that moment, the Count saw their boat for the first time. More than that, he saw Lady Eleanor and Lord Percy, standing on the deck with the Countess between them. Through their field-glasses, Violet and Garth saw the Count twist round in fury. A second later, his expression changed completely. He turned to the other two men, smiling and pointing across the water.

Garth and Violet put down their binoculars thoughtfully. 'I don't know about you,' said Garth, 'but I think we've just seen a man who wasn't expecting to see his wife again.'

Violet nodded. 'You're right. I think he *did* leave her behind on purpose.'

Garth stared at Violet's shocked face. 'I don't want to sound dumb or anything but—'

'But what?'

'But we're going to have to be very, very careful from now on. *Especially* if we are going to trap this man on our own.'

Violet nodded and, without thinking, touched her little finger. She was thinking of what the Count had done to Nicholas as a warning. What would he do to her if he found out she had heard him in the burial chamber, stealing artifacts? And that she could describe the stolen panther in detail to prove it. Her heart banged in her chest.

'What shall we do?' she whispered.

'Play dumb,' replied Garth firmly. 'For Nicholas's sake, as well as our own.'

Garth watched as the Count's *dehabiyah* unfurled its sails and tacked across the river so it could pull up alongside the *Dongola*.

Violet watched her mother's face as she stared at the necklace of crocodiles. She wrinkled her nose. 'Excuse me, Countess, but I do call that rather excessive,' she said. 'I mean, what on earth would one *do* with ten of the brutes?'

'Handbags, shoes and trophies,' replied Lord Percy smoothly. Neither of them was aware that Garth and Violet were only a few feet away and could hear everything they said.

Lord Percy turned to the Countess, who hadn't spoken since the moment they had come on deck and seen the Count on the shore. 'Come along, my dear. We'll have a little celebration when they arrive.'

'Of course,' said the Countess, in a voice so low it could barely be heard. 'I'll just go and refresh myself.' She staggered towards the stairs and disappeared below deck.

Lady Eleanor threw her husband a puzzled look. Usually she was the first to recognise the need for a celebration. Champagne was her favourite drink. Nevertheless, the Countess's reticence over the past week had been rather peculiar. 'Percy . . .' she said, hesitantly.

Lord Percy looked into his wife's exquisite face. 'Yes, my dear?'

'It's odd, I know, but I somehow don't think the Countess is quite as pleased as you think.' Lady Eleanor looked down at her hands in a confused way. 'Indeed, she seems to have been rather cast down by the whole episode.' She paused. 'The truth is, I believe she thinks she was abandoned on purpose.'

'Nonsense,' replied Lord Percy firmly. 'I'm sure it was no more than a misunderstanding. Doubtless the messenger boy's mistake.' He smiled. 'At any rate, nothing that a glass of cold champagne won't settle!'

Lady Eleanor let herself be swayed by her husband's confidence. She had never known him to be wrong. She swept off down the companionway, her fine lawn skirts flying behind her, to arrange for the champagne to be placed on ice. Lord Percy looked out once more across the water at the approaching boat, then followed his wife below.

'Holy cow!' whispered Garth. 'I just thought!'

'What?'

'What if the other woman is with him?'

Violet's eyes widened. 'Do think the Countess suspects that?'

'I'm sure she does,' replied Garth. He looked away to hide a blush. 'It could explain why the Count left her behind.'

'Of course,' said Violet in a matter-of-fact voice. 'But I think there's more to it than a change of partner.'

Garth went purple. 'Uh, yeah. I think you're right.'

Violet watched as the faces on the approaching boat grew clearer. Apart from the Count and his two friends, there appeared to be no other Europeans, and certainly no sign of a woman. Then again, it would be inconceivable for her to show herself in public. Violet's stomach turned over. Perhaps she was hiding below!

On her shoulder, Homer chattered in her ear and tugged at her good-luck necklace. It was almost as if he was trying to talk to her. Violet laughed and stroked his tail. 'Maybe I should send Homer over to look for our mysterious lady!'

Garth rolled his eyes. 'You and that monkey. Anyone would think he could understand English.'

Violet was amazed by the Count's extraordinary performance when he finally came aboard the *Dongola*. When he saw the Countess, he embraced her tenderly and his expressions of relief knew no bounds. He assured her he had sent daily messages to Cairo to inquire of her whereabouts and, when he had not heard, had presumed she was safe and comfortable at Shepheard's and set sail without her.

He reached out and patted his wife's hand. 'The Countess has always been a woman of independence and conviction,' he said, smiling at Lord Percy. 'The truth is, she doesn't approve of my little hobby, you know.'

He introduced the two men with him as Edwin Malory and Montague Cooper. They confirmed his story, joking that the Count's concern for his wife had affected his shooting, otherwise they would have bagged even more crocodiles.

Montague Cooper glanced sideways at the Count and smiled. 'But of course, Count, now that your dear lady has been, uh, recovered, I'm sure your eye will be unflinchingly accurate once more.'

The Count bowed but didn't respond to the compliment.

Violet sipped her lemonade and watched the Count with increasing revulsion. She had seen the Countess flinch as he touched her. As for his so-called companions, she was sure the one called Edwin Malory had been with him in the tomb. She recognised his voice. She felt her knees begin to tremble at the memory of the darkness and the terror of being trapped underground.

'Gracious, Violet,' cried Lady Eleanor. 'You suddenly look quite pale. Are you well?'

'Very well, thank you, Mama.' She forced herself to smile. 'It's only that I'm rather fond of crocodiles. They are beautiful and only ask to be left alone.' She stood up. 'Perhaps some fresh air will do me good.'

'My dear!' cried the Count. 'You must not feel sorry for the brutes. Really, they are just scavengers and killers.'

Violet looked into the man's colourless eyes. 'Perhaps,' she said. 'But it seems to me that the Nile is full of such creatures.' She turned away, her heart pounding at her rudeness, and made her excuses to the Countess. As she looked into the woman's face, she saw it was frozen with terror. It was clear she dreaded joining her husband. Violet made a decision. Turning back she said, 'Indeed, Mama, I am forming an opinion that shooting crocodiles is purely a man's sport. I believe the Countess might prefer to watch the slaughter from a distance.'

Lady Eleanor raised her eyebrows at her daughter's bold suggestion. In any other circumstances, she would have admonished her for being so indiscreet and outspoken. But she too had noticed the Countess's distress, and the same thought had occurred to her. Lady Eleanor's problem had been how to put the offer in such a way that it didn't offend the Count. Violet had done it for her.

'Bravo!' cried Lady Eleanor brightly, as if nothing untoward had been suggested. 'I do believe Violet is right!' She turned pointedly to the Countess. 'We would be delighted if you wished to continue your journey with us and leave the gentlemen to their pleasure. Why, it is only a day or two to Luxor, then we shall all be heading back to Cairo on the train.'

The Count frowned and a flicker of anger passed over his face. He looked quickly down at his khaki hunting breeches and polished knee-boots.

'What a civilised suggestion, my dear,' said Lord Percy smoothly. He nodded to a servant to refill the glasses. 'And one that I am sure would suit both parties.' He turned to the Countess. 'What do you say, my dear lady? It would be an honour to have your company a little longer.'

He turned to the Count and his eyes twinkled. 'I dare say, sir, our accommodation is slightly more suitable for ladies.'

Garth watched this exchange in amazement. Even Violet was stunned by her father's ability to wrong-foot the Count in such a way that for him to insist on his wife's company would make him appear ill-mannered.

Just then, Violet spotted Homer through the window, sitting on the rail of the Count's *dehabiyah*. Something bright dangled from his paws. Her stomach turned over. It was vital that no one else saw him. Whatever he held in his hand could be crucial evidence. It *could* be worthless too, but she couldn't take the chance.

'A rat! A rat!' Violet screamed at the top of her voice. Then she ran up the steps onto the deck. Before anyone could follow her, Homer leapt across from the Count's boat onto the ropes beside her, then climbed onto her shoulder. Violet grabbed what turned out to be a jewel-encrusted lady's watch and dropped it down the front of her dress.

She could have kissed him!

Out of the corner of her eye, she saw the codfish running along the deck towards her with outstretched arms. Violet had never been so glad to see her. It was the perfect cover to escape to her cabin.

'*Violette!*' cried Madame. 'What is this screaming? And your face is so pale. You must lie down on your bed! I shall inform Her Ladyship immediately.'

Violet allowed herself to be led towards her cabin before the adults had time to emerge on deck.

Thank goodness her codfish was such an old French fusspot!

Twenty minutes later, when Violet was supposed to be safely asleep, Garth tapped four times at her door.

'That was quite a rat!' he said, holding his hands wide apart and grinning. He sat down on a chair. 'What did you *really* see?'

Violet fished under her pillow and held up the jewelled watch. 'Homer had this. He took it from the Count's boat. Look at the back.'

Garth turned the watch over. *Tamara. St. Petersburg, 1894* was engraved on the back.

'Do you think it belongs to the woman we heard in the tomb?' said Violet.

'You mean the veiled lady?' asked Garth.

Violet nodded. 'It must be the same person.'

Garth chewed his lip. 'Then it's very unlikely she's on that boat. She'd never have left such an expensive watch behind.'

He jerked his head to where Homer was watching them from inside his cage. His head was cocked and he seemed to be listening. 'Lucky for us, Homer found it.'

Homer chattered and rattled his bars.

'See,' said Violet. 'You were right. He does understand English.'

Garth pulled a face. 'Oh, shut up and be serious!'

Violet looked at the watch. She didn't know much about gems, but the emeralds and diamonds which encircled the watch-face must be worth a fortune. 'She'll be cross she forgot this.'

'It might be just the break we need to find Nicholas,' said Garth, slowly.

Violet frowned. 'What do you mean?'

'That woman was with the Count when I saw the Arab boy following them. I'd say whatever he knows, she knows.'

'Then we have to track her down.'

'First we have to find out who she is.'

Violet put the watch safely under her pillow. 'What was said after I left?'

'The Count was all for following you on deck immediately, but your father stalled him. Probably to give you a chance to disappear.' Garth shook his head. 'I wouldn't be surprised if he saw Homer too. You were both on the same side of the saloon. Anyway, he said you had had an attack of the vapours, then changed the subject to sandstorms.'

'What about the Countess?' asked Violet. 'Will she stay with us?'

Garth nodded. 'Until both boats reach Luxor. Apparently there's a comfortable hotel there.'

'Did the Count seem pleased?'

'No.' Garth grinned at the memory of the Count's black, angry face. 'But he had no choice. You heard what your father said.'

A chill went through Violet. 'I think the Countess is in real danger, Garth. That revolting man was hoping to leave her behind, and now she's surplus to requirements and he's got to deal with her. Not only that, she's looked terrified from the moment she saw him.'

Garth nodded. 'Your mother noticed that, too. No doubt that's why she didn't dismiss you for suggesting the Countess stay with us.' He wrinkled his nose. 'Apart from anything else, the smell of those dead crocodiles was dreadful.' He looked across at Violet's pale face and realised that even though she had played her part brilliantly, just seeing the Count had really shaken her.

'There's something I don't understand though,' said Garth. 'If he abandoned her, why did she want to follow him? Why did she come onto our boat? Wouldn't it have been easier to stay at Shepheard's?'

'Maybe she couldn't afford to stay at Shepheard's,' said Violet. 'I wouldn't be surprised if the Count lives on lies and promises. Besides, a woman without her husband is in an impossible situation. She had to catch up with him. If nothing else, to come to some arrangement with him.'

Garth shook his head. 'I've never met such a brute.'

'Nor have I.' Violet fixed Garth with fierce eyes. 'We're going to trap him, Garth. We really are. All we need is a little more time.'

'And some firm evidence,' muttered Garth.

Neither spoke.

Violet thought again of the crocodiles' carcasses. They were like huge dead dragons on the beach. It was terrible to kill such animals for sport. It wasn't like her father shooting grouse. He only killed what they could eat.

Suddenly Violet felt tired and shivery. 'You'd better leave now, Garth,' she said. 'The codfish is coming back with some tonic for me and if she finds you here, she'll make you drink some, too.'

# TEN

The next morning Violet woke to sunlight creeping around the edge of her curtains. She sat up. Normally she would have jumped out of bed, ready for the excitements of the day, but for some reason her arms ached and her legs felt heavy and lifeless.

All night Violet had tossed and turned, unable to get to sleep and, for the first time since arriving on the boat, she longed for a room in a hotel with a proper bath. Now she swung herself slowly out of her bunk and dressed with fingers that felt as if they were thumbs.

The codfish had left a small breakfast tray out for her with a thermos of tea, some dates and a plate of biscuits. Any other morning, Violet would have grabbed a handful of dates and stuffed the biscuits in her mouth, but this morning she wasn't hungry and the idea of tea made her feel sick. She took down her sun-hat from its hook by the door and went out on deck.

Hannan was at the tiller and both sails were full. He waved when he saw her and pointed upriver. 'Luxor! Missy V! Luxor!'

Violet stared ahead and saw what looked like a small town glinting pink-and-orange in the early morning light. It was such a long time since she had seen so many buildings, she felt a fizz of excitement spread through her.

She looked around and realised she was alone. Everyone else must still be having breakfast. 'I'll tell His Lordship!' she called back to Hannan.

The little man nodded, and Violet went down the short flight of stairs into the dining room, where her father and Garth were sitting opposite each other at the table. She was about to tell them about seeing Luxor, when she noticed the serious expressions on their faces and noticed the plate of uneaten food in front of the Countess's chair. Lady Eleanor wasn't there – she always had breakfast in bed.

'What's happened?' cried Violet. 'What's wrong?'

'The Countess has disappeared, Violet,' said Garth, in a halting voice. He swallowed. 'I saw them take her last night.'

'Tell me again what you heard,' said Lord Percy. There was an urgency in his voice which made Violet realise that he was very worried indeed.

Garth went over the events of the previous night. He had been half asleep, so it wasn't until the morning when he had learned of the Countess's disappearance, that he realised he had seen her being abducted. 'All I can remember is watching two men carrying something that looked like a rolled-up carpet between them along the deck,' he said.

'Were they natives?' asked Lord Percy.

Garth nodded. 'That's why I didn't think any more about it. I presumed they were crew moving something for Hannan.'

'Did *they* see *you*?'

Garth shook his head. 'I was sleeping behind a pile of sails.'

'I don't understand!' cried Violet. 'The Countess would never have allowed herself to be manhandled in such a way!'

Garth and Lord Percy exchanged glances.

'Tell me!' demanded Violet. Her voice was shrill and edgy. Lord Percy looked at his daughter and decided to tell her the truth.

'You're right, Violet. The Countess would have cried out. But –' he paused and chose his words carefully '– I am of the opinion, that she had been rendered unconscious.'

Violet's eyes widened. 'You mean someone drugged her?'

Lord Percy didn't want to upset his daughter any more than was absolutely necessary. 'It's possible. I don't know; but don't worry, my dear,' he said in a firm voice. 'There's an explanation for everything.' He sipped at a small cup of bitter coffee. 'Nevertheless, the sooner we reach Luxor the—'

'We're almost there!' interrupted Violet. 'That's what I came down to tell you.'

'Shall I ask for them at the Hotel Cataract?' said Garth.

'They won't be staying there, Garth,' said Lord Percy, slowly. 'But the staff there will know whether they boarded the morning train to Cairo.'

'The Count is a nasty, evil man!' said Violet suddenly.

'That doesn't make him a kidnapper.' Lord Percy put down his coffee. 'Indeed, he would be quite within his rights to accuse us of interfering in his domestic arrangements.'

Neither Violet nor Garth believed him, but they said nothing. There was no need. It was obvious that Lord Percy didn't believe a word of what he was saying either.

Later that day, they arrived in Luxor. After the peaceful journey by riverboat, the noise and bustle of the quay and the furnace-like heat of the land made them all feel weak and distracted.

Lord Percy immediately ordered a cart to take Madame, Violet and her mother up to the Hotel Cataract. He and Garth would make their way later, asking questions of anyone who might have seen the Count's *dehabiyah* tie up or even sail on to Aswan.

But there was no sign of the Count and his party. No one had seen a *dehabiyah* pass by and everyone agreed that no captain would sail at night, no matter how much he was paid. There was too much shallow water.

Furthermore, no one had seen a party of foreigners board the train for Cairo. The only European who had passed through recently had been a woman on her own.

'When was that?' Garth asked the Arab boy carrying his luggage to the hotel. Lord Percy had gone off to the telegraph office on business. The boy shrugged and held out his hand. Garth put a coin into it.

'Two day back.'

'Did anyone hear her name?' Garth asked, on a whim.

The boy remembered the name because he'd thought it strange for a lady. He had heard the servant girl with her say it distinctly. 'Madam

Tomorrow,' he replied, grinning broadly.

Garth felt his stomach go cold. So the mysterious woman had been and gone long before the Count met them on the Nile. And now she was on her way back to Cairo. What if she left the country? There was no time to lose!

'The Count and his party *must* be on their way back to Cairo,' declared Lady Eleanor later, quite out of sorts over the whole episode. 'I think we should return immediately and notify the police.'

She was sitting in the dining room of the Hotel Cataract with Garth and Lord Percy. Garth had pushed his food around his plate all the way through lunch. His appetite had disappeared. The information he now knew about the other woman weighed heavily on his mind. If they could find her, they might be able to find Nicholas. Garth wanted to tell Lord Percy, but he couldn't without speaking to Violet first. And Violet had come down with a chill and was resting in her bedroom.

Lady Eleanor stood up. 'I shall speak to Madame.

If Violet is well enough, we will take the afternoon train.'

Five minutes later, Violet sat up in bed and assured her mother that she was well enough to catch the train. Madame frowned, but agreed. At least Violet would be able to see a proper foreign doctor in Cairo, should she need to.

Lady Eleanor returned quickly to the saloon. She hated visiting sick-rooms. The idea of catching a disease terrified her. She bolstered herself with a glass of mint tea and admired the view from the hotel roof, while all the bags were loaded onto a donkey cart.

'The Count and those men must have disguised themselves somehow,' said Garth, as he and Violet sat in the back of a bumpy cart on their way to the station. '*And* they had the Countess with them. I think that Tamara woman arranged it.'

Violet tried to make herself think clearly but it was exhausting just watching the crowds of chattering people running about, like so many ants on a nest. She nodded and said nothing.

*

The train carriages were hot and airless and, even though Lord Percy had taken over two first-class cabins and specially fitted boxes had been filled with ice cubes to cool the air, Violet began to feel increasingly ill. Now that she knew from Garth that the mysterious woman had left Luxor, her worries for the Countess increased. It had been foolish to think they could take on someone as ruthless as the Count. Perhaps it *would* be better to do as Garth suggested and tell her father everything they knew.

'Are you holding up, Vi?' Garth asked, looking sideways at Violet's pale, blotchy face. Madame had just left the carriage to find some more drinking water.

Violet groaned and rubbed a hand across her forehead, but didn't speak.

Garth suddenly realised that she was very unwell indeed. 'Violet,' he said in a frightened voice. 'Don't move. I'm going to fetch Madame Poisson.'

'I'm perfectly well, Garth.' Violet pulled a face. 'It's just—' She slumped sideways on the plush banquette and her eyes rolled back into her head.

\*

Violet stood buried up to her neck in hot sand. The sun blazed down on her head out of a cloudless sky. In front of her, the sickly brown waters of the Nile glinted through the reeds. There was a rustling noise and the reeds wobbled. Six enormous crocodiles lumbered towards her. Their shiny yellow bellies bulged on either side of their stubby legs. Slime-crusted teeth glistened like dirty daggers in their cavernous mouths. And all the while their eyes glittered like gold coins. Violet screamed, but only a small, weak sound came from her throat. She screamed again.

The crocodiles came nearer. Now Violet could smell their breath. It smelt dead and musty, like the inside of a tomb. The crocodiles were all around her now. All she could see was the hot, black holes of their open mouths. She twisted and turned in the sand. It burned and rubbed and became hotter and hotter.

The crocodiles were upon her. With every ounce of life left in her, Violet screamed for the last time . . .

'*Violette! Violette!*'

Violet felt something damp and cold being pressed to her forehead. Something hard forced her lips and teeth apart, and a cool, bitter liquid trickled down her throat.

She felt herself tumble over a cliff like a rag-doll as a voice echoed around her. *Violette! Violette! Ah! Mon Dieu!*

Violet woke to find herself back in her attic room at Shepheard's Hotel. Garth was sitting beside her, reading yet another *Sherlock Holmes* adventure.

'Gor blimey,' he said, in a dreadful imitation of a cockney accent. 'You was right poorly, lass.'

Violet sat up on her elbows. 'How long have I been here?'

'Two days.' Garth shut his book.

'*What?*'

'Yup! It was a real drama. Your mother has been prostrate in her room. Then your fish-head lost her temper with the doctor who was looking after you and threw him out.' Garth grinned and cracked his knuckles. 'Boy, that haddock-brain has a good line in French swearwords when she needs them!'

'For heaven's sake, Garth,' Violet said, laughing. 'It's *codfish*. Her name's *codfish*.' As she spoke, she realised she felt almost completely better – and very, very hungry.

'Okay. Okay. Anyway, your codfish took over, mixed up her own medicines and, hey presto, yesterday you turned the corner.' He stood up and pulled back her curtains. 'Nothing sloppy or sentimental, of course, but boy, am I glad you're back!'

Violet laughed. 'I'm glad I'm back, too.'

A ray of sunlight caught the edge of a brass lamp and turned it gold. Suddenly Violet was reminded of the crocodiles' eyes in her dream.

'Garth,' she cried. 'I've just remembered this terrible dream I had.'

'Tell me,' said Garth. He sat down beside her. 'Quickly, before sting-ray comes back.'

When Violet had finished telling him her dream, Garth stared at her with a wide, astonished look in his eyes.

'What do you make of it?' asked Violet.

Garth shook his head, as if he was trying to think straight but couldn't. 'Maybe I'm going mad myself.'

Violet prodded him with a fan that was lying beside her bed. 'What on earth are you talking about?'

'Your dream,' said Garth slowly. He held his head in his hands. 'Remember when we looked in the boxes? Most of the objects that were wrapped in canvas were small.'

'Of course,' said Violet. She borrowed one of his most irritating phrases. 'So what?'

Garth paced back and forth. 'So, ever since I saw that Arab gutting those crocodiles on the beach, I've been thinking. I know lots of people bring back hunting trophies but *no one* brings back that many. At first I thought the Count probably sold them off to people who wanted to pretend they'd killed them themselves. But that didn't make sense either. You wouldn't sell them for that much and it's a complicated job to gut them and preserve them.'

'So what?' said Violet again. 'I don't understand what you're getting at.'

Garth turned and stared at her. 'I don't think those crocs are trophies. I think they're packing cases.'

'What?' Violet sat up in bed. 'Are you feeling cold and shivery by any chance?'

'Listen,' said Garth. 'It's not as crazy as you think. The Count kills as many crocodiles as he needs, gets them properly gutted and then he ships them home.' Garth paused. '*Stuffed to the gills with small artifacts wrapped in greaseproof canvas!*'

Garth swung the brass light around so golden sunbeams flashed around the room like fireworks. '*Now* do you think I'm crazy?'

Violet stared at him. 'You're right!' she shouted. 'Who would suspect anything? Garth! You're a genius!' She stopped and her eyes gleamed. 'Now, how are we going to catch him red-handed?'

'Your turn, partner,' said Garth with a grin. 'I've been working hard in my corner.'

Normally, Violet would have said something back, but she was thinking so fast she barely heard him.

'Okay!' she said 'I think I've got it! At least it's a start.'

'Shoot!' replied Garth, looking anxiously at the door.

'We need to find a shipping agent. They'll know what steamers are leaving Alexandria for England. Garth!' Violet clapped her hands. 'We've got him!'

'Now all we have to do is find Nicholas,' said Garth, slowly.

'Once the police have got the Count, they'll force him to tell us where Nicholas is.'

'I hope you're right,' replied Garth. 'At any rate, we've got to get going before those crocodiles are crated up in the hold of a boat and halfway home.'

The door flew open and Madame strode into the room. '*Violette!* What are you doing sitting up? Lie down immediately!' She glared at Garth. 'This is your fault, young man. Don't you understand? *Violette* is recovering from a dangerous fever.'

'I've recovered,' said Violet, taking her governess's hand. 'And Garth has just told me it's all thanks to you.'

'*Mais pas du tout. Mais pas du tout,*' murmured

Madame. 'You are a strong girl. You would have recovered anyway.'

'But not so quickly,' replied Garth, gallantly.

Violet slid down under the covers. 'See, it's not Garth's fault,' she said quickly. 'He came to visit me and I asked him to fetch me some –' she realised she had no idea what time it was '– uh, breakfast.'

Violet looked up through her lashes, aware that Garth was watching her with an amazed expression on his face. 'Now that I'm better, may I have Homer with me? I do get so lonely recovering on my own.'

Madame's mouth set in a firm line. 'Certainly not! Heaven knows what germs that little beast is carrying.'

There was a knock on the door. A turbanned servant boy walked in with a cage containing Homer. The monkey shrieked and jumped up and down on his bar when he saw Violet.

'Your father, he send,' said the boy, beaming. 'He say monkey help you get better.'

The room was thick with tension. Garth decided this was a good time to leave. He nodded to Violet. 'I'm going to find Ahmed in the bazaar.'

'Not *another* monkey!' cried Madame, in a horrified voice.

'Ask him if he has heard anything of Nicholas,' said Violet quickly.

'I already have and he hasn't heard a thing.'

Violet's face fell and she stared down at her bedclothes. Even though they now knew how the Count smuggled his treasure out of Egypt, it would still be a few days before they could track him down. And, for all they knew, he might have decided to get rid of both Nicholas and the Countess before he left.

'Now look what you've done,' cried Madame, watching Violet's face. 'Off you go right now! *Violette* needs to rest.'

Violet struggled to sit up but Garth could see that Madame was right. It would be at least another day before Violet was well enough to leave her bed.

'Don't worry,' said Garth gently. 'Ahmed says bad news travels fast in Cairo.'

'I hope he's right,' said Violet quietly. 'Come and see me when you get back.'

'You can count on it.' Garth shut the door behind him.

'Now, *Violette*—' began Madame Poisson.

Violet held up her hand. 'Please, Madame. I would like my breakfast.'

'It's noon, *ma chérie*,' replied Madame, as she plumped up Violet's pillows.

Violet smiled and shrugged. 'Then I shall have a light luncheon.'

# ELEVEN

Ahmed wasn't at his stall in the covered square. When Garth asked where he was, the young Arab who had taken his place rolled his eyes and shook his head. It was a stupid question, of course. Garth knew that. Even if Ahmed was five feet away around a corner, the boy wouldn't have told him. He decided to wait in the tearoom where he had met Nicholas the night they had returned to buy Homer. The same night the Count had first seen them together.

Garth settled himself into a corner of the crowded room. Opposite him, a group of men were sitting cross-legged on cushions, smoking a sweet-smelling tobacco through a long, bendy tube which passed through a bowl of water. Nicholas had explained that the steam from the water made the tobacco taste smoother. At the time, an old man had grinned toothlessly at him and passed over the tube. Garth had refused, preferring mint tea to smoke.

That all seemed a long time ago now.

'Mr Garth!'

Garth spun around to see Ahmed standing bright-eyed and grinning in front of him.

'Ahmed! Who told you I was here?'

Ahmed smiled wider. 'My brother. He knows everything.'

Garth motioned to a cushion in front of him and Ahmed sat down. 'Have you heard anything more about Nicholas?'

'No. But the man with the bad eyes has been seen in the bazaar.'

Garth's heart lurched. So the Count *was* back in Cairo. 'We have to find Nicholas,' he cried insistently.

Ahmed raised his eyebrows but said nothing. These foreigners were so excitable.

Garth banged down his teacup. 'I think . . . I think the Count might kill him!'

Ahmed sipped at his own tea. 'My uncle has also seen this bad man coming away from Mr Spiro,' he said, ignoring Garth's outburst. 'His office is very near your hotel.'

Garth tried to control himself. He *had* to calm down. This was Egypt. If there was a chance of finding Nicholas alive, they had to do it Ahmed's way. 'Who is Mr Spiro?'

'He is a fat man who sails ships across the sea from Alexandria.'

Garth forgot himself. 'A shipping agent!' he cried, slopping tea on his lap. 'Violet said we should look for someone like that!'

'A clever young lady,' agreed Ahmed, solemnly.

'Ahmed,' said Garth, more calmly now. 'How can we find out what the Count was arranging with Mr Spiro?'

Ahmed rubbed his fingers and thumb together. 'That's easy. A bribe. But he won't tell you and he won't tell me.'

'We *have* to find Nicholas,' said Garth again.

'He's our only hope.' As he spoke, he saw a guilty expression pass over Ahmed's face.

'I do have news of Nicholas,' said Ahmed at last. 'But it is not good.'

Garth could barely bring himself to ask the question on his lips. 'Is he dead?'

'By now? Quite possibly.' Ahmed looked into Garth's horrified face. Though they were almost the same age, it seemed to Ahmed that the young American was more like his youngest of brothers. 'You see, my father discovered that Nicholas was kidnapped. But not by the Count. By Gumrhaddin, the Turk.'

'You mean the merchant?' asked Garth incredulously. 'The slave-trader?'

Ahmed nodded. 'The same disgusting specimen, yes. But he did not want to sell Nicholas. He wanted to keep him as insurance against the Count not keeping his end of the bargain and giving him some of the artifacts he stole. Gumrhaddin knows that Nicholas has much secret knowledge of the Count's activities and that the Count would pay for his silence.'

Garth's head was spinning. 'How do you *know* all of this? And why didn't you tell me the truth when I asked yesterday?'

'I didn't tell you because my father said no. You see, Garth, my whole family works for Nicholas. My father worked for his father. We have always been in business together. Besides, we were hoping to gain Nicholas's release yesterday so he would be able to go straight to the protection of Lord Percy at the Shepheard's Hotel.'

Garth didn't ask how Lord Percy was involved. He knew he would be wasting his breath. Ahmed would never tell him. Besides it was all sounding complicated enough already.

Ahmed stuck his finger in the little brass cup and scooped up some soggy sugar crystals. 'The problem is that now the Count has handed over Gumrhaddin's share of the stolen artifacts, Nicholas is no longer useful to the Turk. And, of course, the Count would be only to pleased to get rid of him once and for all.'

Garth's face went white.

'Exactly,' said Ahmed grimly. 'Nicholas

169

disappeared from Gumrhaddin's cellar last night. A day after the Count returned to Cairo.' He paused. 'I will not hide it from you, Garth. I am worried for Nicholas now. All my family are out looking for him.'

Nicholas Etherington shuffled quickly down the crowded street. He knew he must keep his footsteps small and dainty. Arab women never took long strides. However, even though he was dressed from head to foot in a flowing, black *burka* with only a square of fine netting to see through, he was still far too tall and it was difficult to hide his large hands under the cloth. Anyone looking at him twice would know that he wasn't a woman.

Nicholas tried to breathe as normally as possible. He fell into step behind a donkey cart piled high with stripey green watermelons, hoping the wheels and donkey-legs might camouflage him. The Count's spies would be looking for him everywhere. And it didn't take a genius to work out that he would head for Shepheard's Hotel.

Ahead of him to the right was the famous long

terrace, with its palm trees and rattan tables and chairs laid out to look over the busy street. The donkey cart turned away and Nicholas quickened his step towards the hotel. His next problem would be how to get past the doormen.

Nicholas swallowed and tried to make a plan. He knew these things were a matter of luck and judgement. He had been fortunate enough to be carrying a small quantity of jewels the night he had been kidnapped by Gumrhaddin's men. He had bought them especially to take with him the next day when he was due to join the Winters on board *Dongola*. Nicholas knew from experience that swapping jewels for artifacts was the easiest way to do business in the desert markets because the dealers didn't want official money. Without those jewels, he could never have bribed one of Gumrhaddin's servants to help him.

Nicholas had been pretty sure he knew the reason for his imprisonment, which had meant he was safe enough until the Count returned. And he knew he would never catch the Count red-handed if he tried to escape the moment he was imprisoned. He had had to wait it out and make the Count think he had succeeded in his plan. So, once Nicholas had sent a message to Ahmed, he had passed his time playing cards with his captors and pretending to believe that he would be released as promised. In the meantime, he had bribed the same servant to smuggle in long skirts and a *burka*. With his last jewel, he had bought the information that he hoped might save his life.

Yesterday, the servant had told him that the Count was expected late that night and that Gumrhaddin was saying he had tired of talking to the foreigner and would be glad to exchange him for a couple more artifacts.

However, the Count's return was unexpectedly early, the servant reported, and Gumrhaddin was edgy. As Nicholas dug a hole to bury his clothes, he wondered what had gone wrong. Suddenly the servant had reappeared. The Count had arrived and was demanding his hostage.

As quickly as he could, Nicholas had pulled on the baggy skirts and pulled the *burka* over his head.

Then he had climbed the stone steps from his underground cell and slipped out of a side door with a duplicate key.

He had had no jewels left to send a message to Ahmed.

It was a warm evening, with a huge full moon. Nicholas decided to make his way as near to Shepheard's Hotel as he dared, and hide himself until morning. Then when the streets were full, he would walk the last half a mile and slip in through the front entrance.

Somehow.

Now the turbanned doormen were watching him suspiciously. They had a quick conversation and were joined a moment later by another man. This one looked bigger and more burly.

Sweat began to run down Nicholas's back. It was obvious the doormen realised he wasn't a woman. They began to move slowly towards him.

At that moment, Garth hurried across the street. Nicholas turned around and found himself staring straight into Garth's eyes.

'Garth!' cried Nicholas, as loudly as he dared. 'Stop! It's me, Nicholas! Come towards me. Don't look surprised! I beg of you!'

At first Garth thought the heat had finally got to him. He was looking at an unusually tall woman in a veil who spoke English like a man. In fact, she was claiming to be the very person he was thinking about. Garth tried to reply but the words stuck in his throat.

'Garth!' cried Nicholas urgently. 'Pull yourself together, boy! I need help!'

Garth stared at the woman's hands and noticed the thick wrists and strong, stubby fingers. At last he was able to speak.

'Nicholas,' he spluttered. 'What do you want me to do?'

'Wave to the doormen,' said Nicholas quickly. 'Then take my arm and lead me through into the garden.'

The doormen watched in amazement as Garth waved and led the tall, veiled lady towards the shadowy gardens at the back of the hotel. One of the doormen made a move towards them, but the other pulled him back. Who were they to question the young gentleman's actions? He was a guest at the hotel. He was entitled to receive what visitors he liked.

Violet looked up from her bathchair, under the shade of a palm tree, and saw Garth leading a large lady across the lawn. What on earth was he doing? She called out and, to her amazement, the two figures turned and almost ran towards her. Garth pulled up two chairs and the strange, veiled woman sat down, panting.

'It's Nicholas,' said a deep voice from behind the veil.

Violet jerked up in her seat and her hand flew to her mouth. 'For heaven's sake!'

'Don't look surprised,' begged Nicholas. 'The Count's spies are everywhere. We have to make a plan – and there's very little time.'

Three hours later, Nicholas stood in Garth's room and stared at himself in the mirror. He was dressed in a striped linen suit that Ahmed had had copied from one that Violet had removed from her father's dressing room earlier. Luckily, Lord and Lady Winters were visiting friends who owned a villa on the edge of the city, and they did not plan to return until the following morning. The chestnut-brown beard Nicholas had grown used to over the past six weeks was gone, as was the usual brown of his own hair. Now he had short, dyed-black hair, parted in the middle, and a tufty, black moustache. Ahmed had found him a pair of thick horn-rimmed spectacles and stuffed one of his shoes with wadding so that he was forced to walk with a slight limp. Nicholas picked up a straw boater and took a last look in the mirror. They had done a good job. He was almost unrecognisable as the young man the Count had seen in the bazaar.

Nicholas opened the door of Garth's room and made his way down from the top floor onto the roof terrace. Violet and Garth were waiting for him at a tea-table laden with cakes and scones. As Nicholas sat down, he realised he hadn't eaten for ages. After three cups of tea, four scones and four slices of lemon cake, his mind began to work properly again.

He glanced around him to make sure they couldn't be heard. Then he leant forward in his chair. 'Violet. Can you tell me again the three words you heard the Count say in the tomb?'

Violet put down her cup. The relief of knowing Nicholas was safe and a very large lunch earlier in the day seemed to have brought about a full recovery. As for Nicholas's disguise, even Madame hadn't recognised him when Garth had introduced her to Gerald Ferguson, recently arrived from Holland. Violet could have clapped her hands with delight. Everything was going very well indeed. Now all they had to do was trap the Count. After that Nicholas could hand him over to the Egyptian police, who would force him to tell them what he had done with the Countess.

'Crocodiles, gold and star,' Violet said quickly.

Nicholas put one more piece of scone into his mouth. 'Well, we know what the first two mean.' He swallowed a large mouthful of tea. 'I shall have to pay a visit to that shipping agent Ahmed mentioned.' Nicholas frowned. 'Blast.'

'What's the problem?' asked Garth.

'No money,' said Nicholas in an exasperated voice. 'I'll need to bribe that Spiro fellow and I can't get any funds from my bank. Not looking like this, anyway.'

Violet reached into her pocket and pulled out a small purse. 'Sorry, I forgot. Ahmed gave me this to give to you.'

Nicholas grinned. 'That boy will run this country, one day, I swear it!' He took the purse. 'I'll be back in a hour. Where shall I meet you?'

'At the back of the garden,' replied Violet. 'Where I was before. You can't see it from the hotel.'

Nicholas nodded and set off down the terrace steps.

Garth and Violet picked up their teacups and watched Nicholas make his way, limping slightly, through the crowds.

Their hands froze in mid-air.

The Count was climbing down from a small trap on the street. He threw a coin at the boy driving and ordered him to wait. Then he walked up to the hotel entrance.

'Garth!' cried Violet. 'He'll bribe the doormen

and find out everything. You have to warn Nicholas!'

'I can't,' replied Garth. 'The Count knows what I look like. If he saw me running over, it would give Nicholas away.' He stood up and ducked behind a palm tree. 'Let's get out of here. All we can do is wait for him to come back.'

But it wasn't Nicholas who appeared in the garden two hours later. Ahmed jumped out from behind a bush and handed Garth a note. Violet read it over his shoulder.

*In haste. The* Star of Egypt *sails in two days from Alexandria, bound for London.*

Violet gasped. 'That's what the Count was talking about when I heard him say "star"!' She looked up at Garth. 'Now what are we going to do?'

Garth turned to Ahmed and spoke in Arabic. 'Did Mr Etherington have any other message for us?'

Ahmed nodded. 'He would like you to accompany me and my cousin to Cairo station at two o'clock in the morning. We will meet you by the back gate.'

Garth translated quickly.

'I don't think that's a good idea,' said Violet, hesitantly. 'Someone's bound to notice us on the streets at that time of night.'

Garth spoke to Ahmed.

'The young lady is in her right mind,' he replied, grinning. 'For that reason, I will bring you both robes of dark cloth.' He laughed and held up his hands. 'Then you will look just like me!'

When Garth explained to Violet what Ahmed had said, Violet felt a cold shiver pass over her. She was excited and frightened at the same time. She knew they should tell her father, but he wasn't here. And now that Nicholas was back, the possibility that the three of them might trap the Count on their own was irresistible.

'What do you say, Violet?' asked Garth.

Violet could tell from his voice that he was thinking the same way she was.

'I say we'll be at the back gate at two o'clock,' replied Violet.

Garth grinned. 'So do I!'

# TWELVE

The moon hung like a pearl in an inky black sky when Ahmed met Violet and Garth by the gate at the back of the hotel garden. Violet had insisted that Homer come with her and the monkey clung to her neck when he recognised Ahmed's scent.

Ahmed grinned. 'Monkey very useful.' In his hand, he held two Arab costumes in fine black cotton, and Violet and Garth quickly pulled them on over their clothes.

They followed Ahmed through the gate and down an alleyway. Within minutes they had turned left and right a dozen times. Violet swallowed nervously. They would never be able to find their way back on their own.

According to Ahmed, Nicholas would meet them at a warehouse by the train station. This was where all the cargo bound for Alexandria was stored. Nicholas was sure that the Count and his friends would not risk sending such valuable cargo unaccompanied to Alexandria.

'What if he's right?' asked Violet anxiously. 'What will we do if we find them there? We are only four.'

Ahmed grinned and shook his head. 'My brothers are coming too.'

He stopped by a donkey and cart sitting under a palm tree. 'Please, get in. My cousin will take us to the station.'

There was a flash of white teeth in the moonlight. A boy younger than Ahmed jumped down to help Violet up the step. Garth climbed in beside her, but Ahmed insisted on riding up front with his cousin.

Twenty minutes later, they could make out the

loom of the elegant stone building that was Cairo station. The cart slowed and turned up a tiny alleyway so it wouldn't be seen from the road. Ahmed and his cousin jumped down. 'Now, we must be very quiet,' whispered Ahmed. He pointed to a cluster of sheds opposite the station. 'Nicholas will be waiting for us.'

The dark cloth of their Arab costumes made the group almost invisible in the night. Violet and Garth followed Ahmed and his cousin as they threaded their way in and out of the shadows, until they came to the remains of a well. Ahmed stopped and peered anxiously around him. 'Nicholas comes here,' he whispered.

Violet looked over at the sheds. They were dark and silent. Suddenly she saw the flicker of a lamp. She touched Garth's hand. 'Look! He's inside!'

'Or someone is,' replied Garth, in a hollow voice.

Once again, Ahmed looked around him. He whispered something to his cousin who nodded and ran, bent double, across to the shed. He peered inside, turned and beckoned them over.

Nothing could have prepared Violet for what she saw next.

In the middle of a huge shed, surrounded by piles and piles of wooden boxes, Nicholas was bent over an open crate. He looked up when he saw them and beckoned. Violet peered into the crate.

Inside was the body of the Countess Maria.

Violet stuffed her fist into her mouth to stifle a scream.

'She's not dead,' said Nicholas quickly. 'But she needs urgent attention. She's been heavily drugged and her pulse is very slow.' He heaved the Countess into a sitting position. Her head lolled on her shoulders and fell backwards.

'I take her,' said Ahmed quickly. 'My uncle has herbs to wake her up.'

Nicholas nodded. Ahmed whistled twice and his cousin appeared beside him.

'It'll need three of us,' muttered Nicholas.

Ahmed lifted the Countess up by her shoulders and his cousin picked up her feet. Nicholas supported her middle. 'I'll be back in a minute,' he said to Garth and pointed to two crowbars on the mud floor. 'Look for crates big enough to hold a crocodile.' He paused grimly. 'The same shape as a coffin.'

Violet watched, horrified, as the three men manhandled the Countess through the door and out into the night. What sort of man would drug his own wife and shut her up in a crate? If he wanted to get rid of her, why hadn't he killed her? Then again maybe he had other plans for her, and in the meantime just wanted to keep her quiet until the artifacts were safely out of the country. But then what?

'Do you think the Count will come back for her?' croaked Violet. She thought she was going to be sick.

'Violet! Come here quickly!' hissed Garth, suddenly.

Violet picked up a lantern and a crowbar and ran over to the corner where he was standing. Behind him Homer was running up and down a long coffin-shaped crate, chattering and baring his teeth.

'Garth!' whispered Violet. 'Do you think the Count—?'

'Shh!' cried Garth. 'I'm sure Homer's found what we're looking for!' He pointed to a row of similar-looking crates. 'See, there are ten of them! One for each crocodile!' He bent down and eased the crowbar under the securely-nailed lid. It was impossible to open.

'Darn it!' muttered Garth. 'I can't do it! We'll have to wait for Nicholas to come back.'

The moment he said this, Violet suddenly realised how long it had been since Nicholas left to help carry the Countess's body to the donkey cart. Something was wrong. He should have been back by now. A cold terror crept over her.

There was the sound of scuffling feet beyond the warehouse door.

Without a word, Garth doused the lantern-flame. The two of them stood, waiting for their eyes to get used to the darkness. For the first time, Violet felt choked by the hot, dusty air of the warehouse.

Voices shouted. One voice was clear above the others. It was the Count.

'Quick!' whispered Garth. 'Before they come in.' He hid their lanterns and the crowbars. Then he hoisted her up onto a pile of crates and jumped up beside her. 'Just as well I couldn't open the crate. Now they won't know we're here.'

'But what can we do?'

'I don't know. But don't make a sound. We'll be crocodile food if they find us.'

Violet felt Homer clamber onto her shoulder and cling to her neck. She wished she had listened to Garth at the beginning and told her father what they knew. Now they were trapped and no one except Ahmed had any idea where they were. And Ahmed didn't know that the Count had returned.

'What have you done with my wife, Etherington?' It was a snarl more than a question. There was a hard *slap* and a grunt. 'How did you track me down? Who's been helping you?'

Another *slap*. Nicholas groaned.

Violet stiffened. Garth squeezed her arm and put his finger to his lips. At least Ahmed had been able to get away with the Countess before this terrible man had returned and overpowered Nicholas.

'You won't get away with it, Dufort,' cried

Nicholas, in a raw voice. 'The police know I'm here.'

'Balderdash!' replied the Count. 'I paid off the Chief yesterday. He won't be bothering with you any more.'

Violet peeked out from behind a crate. In the dull light of the lantern, she saw Nicholas slumped against the wall. The Count was bent over him, tying his hands behind his back. 'If you weren't so stubborn, I would have cut you in,' said the Count in a soft, nasty voice. 'You're clever and I could use someone like you. It's a good living, you know.'

'Especially when you cheat on your partners,' spat Nicholas. 'What have you done with Malory and Cooper?'

The Count laughed. 'Imbeciles. They outlived their usefulness.'

'So you threw them in the river, I suppose.' Suddenly Nicholas realised that if he could keep the Count talking, even if he didn't escape alive, Garth and Violet would be able to tell Lord Percy what they had heard.

'Gumrhaddin has subtler methods,' said the Count, lightly. 'Besides, he owed me one after letting you escape.' As he spoke, he dragged Nicholas to his feet and pulled him towards a coffin-shaped crate just below where Garth and Violet were hiding. Violet watched in horror as the Count threw Nicholas onto the ground and began to prise open the crate. 'What a shame you had to find out the secret of my crocodiles.' He pulled back the lid. 'Not that you'll be able to tell anyone, of course.'

Garth turned to Violet and pointed at a crate that was on top of a stack in front of them. He made pushing movements with his hands. For a moment, Violet didn't understand. Then she saw that the crate was directly above the Count's head. If they could push it fast enough it might knock him over, which might just give Nicholas the chance he needed to save his life. It was a long shot. What if they missed and the Count captured them all? But then, if they didn't try, Nicholas would be murdered in front of them.

They had to risk it. Violet reached for the

pendant at her neck and squeezed it. Garth nodded and crossed his fingers.

'Haven't you forgotten about your wife?' said Nicholas, in a mocking voice. 'When she wakes up, I'd say she'll want to talk to Lord Percy . . .'

The Count snorted. 'Stupid woman. She knows nothing. She thinks I'm a big-game hunter, like everyone else.'

'So why not leave her out of it?'

'She's in the way,' said the Count shortly. 'My plans are with Miss Tolstoy. By the time Maria wakes up, we'll be on our way to London, courtesy of the Star Line.' He pulled Nicholas to his feet. 'That is, after we have attended to a little business in St Petersburg. Miss Tolstoy's father trades in icons.'

'I know Serge Tolstoy,' replied Nicholas smoothly, but Violet heard a note of confusion in his voice. He had got it wrong. The Count and Tamara Tolstoy weren't sailing on the *Star of Egypt*, after all. Now Nicholas was playing for time in earnest.

'Tolstoy's a crook,' sneered Nicholas, trying to

goad the Count into talking. 'But he's well above your class, Dufort. I'd watch out, if I were you. Tolstoy doesn't like sharing. Except with his own family, of course.'

Nicholas paused and played his trump card. 'Have you seen Miss Tolstoy recently? I hear she takes after her father in every way.'

'Shut your filthy mouth!' shouted the Count furiously. 'She's waiting for me in Luxor, if you must know!' Violet watched in horror as he hauled Nicholas over the open crate and pushed him backwards so he fell inside. 'Say your prayers, Etherington!'

The Count took a small pistol out of his pocket.

After that everything happened very quickly.

As if he had understood Garth's plan, Homer suddenly jumped onto the Count's head and clawed at his face.

'What the devil!'

As the Count struggled with the screeching monkey, Garth and Violet shoved the heavy crate forwards. Homer sprang sideways as it landed on the Count's shoulders and knocked him to the ground. Nicholas scrambled out of the crate. 'Grab the pistol!' he shouted, as Garth stared down from their hiding place.

The Count craned backwards to see who was above him but Nicholas kicked him in the chin and knocked him out cold. It was crucial that the Count didn't know who was with him. If Lord Percy ever found out that his daughter, or indeed his ward, had been put in such a dangerous situation, he would never trust Nicholas again. Without them, though, he would never have worked out how the artifacts were being smuggled out. But he knew that the Count would make it his business to track down the culprits the moment he was released from prison and take his revenge. So, it was essential their identity was kept secret – quite apart from the fact that he had sworn to both of them that he would keep their involvement hidden.

'It's all right,' cried Nicholas. Both Violet and Garth were crouching in the shadows, terrified that the Count would recognise them. 'He's unconscious!'

Violet and Garth jumped down. Garth picked

up the pistol and Violet began struggling with the rope that tied Nicholas's wrists.

'Here,' said Garth, handing her the pistol. 'You hold this. I've got a pen-knife in my pocket.'

Violet took the pistol and held it in her hand. It was heavier than she'd expected. Almost in a dream, she turned it towards her to have a better look.

'No!' shouted Nicholas at the top of his voice.

Violet was so surprised, she threw the pistol on the ground.

It went off with a deafening *bang*!

For a split second no one moved. The acrid smell of gunpowder filled the air. It reminded Violet of fireworks.

There was the sound of thudding feet. Suddenly they were surrounded by ten young men, all of whom looked like Ahmed.

'Accident,' said Nicholas. 'No one hurt.' He turned to Ahmed. 'We must leave immediately.'

Ahmed prodded the prone body of the Count. 'What of him, Mr Nicholas? What would you like us to do?'

For a moment, Nicholas held his head in his hands and didn't speak. It was clear the events of the past forty-eight hours had taken their toll. He stumbled backwards and collapsed on the ground.

'I know what to do,' said Violet, in a clear voice. 'Garth and I will go back to the hotel. Bring the Countess to Madame Poisson, as if you found her in the bazaar. As for the Count –' she couldn't bring herself to look at the face of the man on the ground '– keep him prisoner. Lord Percy will deal with him in the morning.'

Garth translated and Ahmed looked at Violet in amazement. The girl seemed so composed. 'And Nicholas, Missy?' he asked.

'I'll look after him in my room,' said Garth to Ahmed. 'Can you get him there unnoticed?'

Ahmed grinned and nodded. 'My brother-in-law is night porter at the hotel.'

Dawn was turning the sky pink and pale orange as Violet pulled off her clothes and jumped into her bed. There was a knock on her door. In his cage, Homer chattered angrily. Violet sighed with relief.

It was only Madame. Homer always made the same noise when she was near.

'*Violette?*' whispered Madame, in a low trembling voice. '*Violette?*'

Homer shook his bars and screeched. '*Shhh!* Homer!' said Violet, in her best sleepy voice. She sat up in bed. 'Madame! Is there something wrong?'

The little French governess sat down at the end of bed. 'Yes, *Violette.* Something dreadful has happened. The Countess . . .' She put her head in her hands. 'Oh, *Violette!* I didn't know what to do. If only your parents were here!'

Violet put out her hand. She felt guilty for upsetting her dear codfish, but there was nothing else she could have done. The Countess had to be placed under her family's protection and Madame was their only adult representative. 'What on earth is going on?' cried Violet.

Then she sat back and listened as Madame described how a servant had come to her door in the middle of the night to tell her that that Countess Kapolski was in the hotel and needed her care immediately.

'She had been drugged, poor woman!' Madame Poisson squeezed Violet's hand. 'Heaven knows where they found her. *Mon Dieu!* I have never known anything like it!'

'Drugged?' cried Violet, as if shocked and amazed. 'How terrible! Where is she now?'

'She is resting,' replied Madame. 'I gave her my salts and a herbal tonic. She will recover. But—'

'But what?'

'The Countess *must* speak with your father, the moment he arrives.' She shook her head again and patted Violet's hand. 'I shouldn't have disturbed you, *ma pauvre.*'

Violet squeezed her governess's hand. 'Go back to bed,' she said gently. 'You need some rest.'

Madame nodded and opened the door. As she left the room, Homer threw back his head and howled with what sounded like glee.

Violet sat out on the great terrace looking down at the wide, dusty street below her. Homer sat on her shoulder, holding the pendant in his hand and turning it over and over. He had become

198

completely obsessed with the shiny turquoise eye. Violet stroked his neck but he didn't look up. She was glad that Nicholas had given her permission to keep the pendant. She remembered his rueful smile. *It's the least I can do to thank you.*

It was barely six-thirty in the morning and already the streets were crowded and there was heat in the sun. Violet lay back on the cushions of her cane chair and rested her arms along the sides. A great feeling of relief washed over her. The Count had been caught. Nicholas was safe. Now all she wanted to do was sit back and enjoy the last few days of her holiday. She watched as a small boy jumped onto the back of a donkey cart and burrowed into a mound of sacks before the driver saw him. She burst out laughing.

'You're in a good mood this morning,' said Garth, behind her.

Violet looked up. 'I do believe I should stay up half the night more often.' She smiled at him and pointed to the seat beside her. 'Or perhaps it was the feel of a pistol in my hand. At any rate, yes, I do feel rather jolly.'

Garth threw himself into the curved rattan chair and fell back against the cushions. 'I could fall asleep at any moment.'

Violet prodded him with her foot. 'Don't you dare.' She waved to a waiter and ordered two large cups of hot chocolate and a plate of almond buns. 'Now, tell me exactly what happened with Nicholas. I presume he isn't still asleep in your room.'

Garth shook his head. 'A full English breakfast and a strong cup of coffee and he made a complete recovery. He left at dawn.'

A smartly painted trap with a black canvas cover stopped outside the hotel entrance. The driver jumped down and opened the door. Lady Eleanor stepped down onto the ground, followed by Lord Percy. Violet couldn't believe her eyes. Her mother never usually rose before ten o'clock in the morning.

Lord Percy's face was serious. They spoke for a moment, and her mother nodded and turned to walk up the steps into the hotel.

Lord Percy jumped back into the trap and it set

off in the direction of the bazaar.

'Where do you think he's going?' asked Violet, nervously.

'He's going to see the Count,' said Garth firmly. 'Nicholas sent Ahmed to him with a message. They have an appointment with the Consul this morning.'

Violet frowned. 'Why the Consul? Shouldn't the Count be in a police cell?'

Garth rubbed his hand over his face. 'Nicholas said they won't trust the Egyptian police now. Besides, there are apparently underground cells at the Consulate.'

Violet raised her eyebrows but didn't speak. She didn't even bother to wonder how Nicholas could have found out that her parents were staying with the Miles-Morgans. You could find out anything you wanted in Cairo if you knew the right people to bribe.

The hot chocolate arrived with a plate of buns and two slices of watermelon. Violet passed one cup over to Garth and lifted up her own. 'Shall we leave it to the adults, now?' She picked up an almond bun and watched Homer's tiny paws close over it. 'The exciting part is over.'

Garth held out his cup. 'Here's to ya, partner. It's been great doin' business together.'

Violet laughed. 'Let's make it a habit.' She held out her own cup and spoke in a New York accent. 'Whaddya say?'

Garth swallowed his hot chocolate in one noisy, satisfying slurp.

He grinned and replied in fluent, aristocratic English. 'Two minds but with a single thought, my dear.'

Violet picked up a bun and threw it at him.